JESSICA BECK

THE DONUT MYSTERIES, BOOK 44

SIFTED SENTENCES

Donut Mystery 44: SIFTED SENTENCES

The First Time Ever Published!

The 44th Donut Mystery.

Jessica Beck is the *New York Times* Bestselling Author of the Donut Mysteries, the Cast Iron Cooking Mysteries, the Classic Diner Mysteries, the Ghost Cat Cozy Mysteries, and more.

WHEN SUZANNE'S MOTHER gets a threatening note, no one but Suzanne and Grace seems to take it seriously. After all, several other folks around town have gotten them, too. The police think it's all just one big prank, but Suzanne knows better. As she and her best friend begin to dig into the case, things suddenly turn fatal in April Springs when someone is murdered, and Suzanne must figure out whether the threat against Momma is a separate incident or if it's tied into the same goal of getting rid of her mother once and for all!

Always and forever,
To P and E

Prologue

IT WAS LATE IN THE afternoon, and the petite older woman had her back to the street as she paused to stare at something in the bushes in Myra Hickering's front yard, so she never saw the car as it left the road and suddenly sped toward her.

The truth was that she never stood a chance.

The impact sent her flying through the air straight into Myra's concrete birdbath, and the assassin's car was gone before the lifeless body even hit the ground. Unfortunately, the impact with the birdbath left her face almost completely unrecognizable.

It was a sad day in April Springs.

They'd just lost one of their own.

Chapter 1
Earlier That Day

"WHAT ARE YOU DOING here at this time of day?" I asked my mother as I locked the door of my donut shop behind me. I'd dismissed my assistant, Emma, from Donut Hearts twenty minutes earlier, since she had a special session of one of her classes at the college she didn't want to be late for. I'd volunteered to finish up her tasks as well as mine, an offer she'd been more than happy to accept. In addition to the keys gripped in one hand, I had the bank deposit tucked under that arm and a box of assorted donuts left over from the day clutched in the other. It made for quite the juggling act getting everything locked up, but this wasn't my first rodeo.

"Why on earth are you so surprised to see me, Suzanne? Can't a mother visit her daughter at work for no particular reason?" she asked plaintively. Momma was petite, but I pitied anyone who underestimated the size of her spirit. Inside, she was a sumo wrestler.

"She can, but she usually doesn't," I answered with a grin. "Care for a donut?"

"No, thank you." Momma was thin—unlike me, her big-boned daughter—and it was tough to tempt her with *any* of my treats, but that never stopped me from offering them.

"How about taking them home to Phillip, then? Oh, that's right. He's on a quest. How is his trip going so far? Have you heard from him lately?"

"As a matter of fact, I received a telephone call from him last night," my mother admitted. "He told me that the trip was doing him a world of good, though he still feels a bit guilty about abandoning me so soon after getting the good news about his diagnosis. It took him three long months to get back on his feet again after the surgery, and as soon as he found out there were no traces of cancer left, he took off."

My stepfather had undergone surgery for intermediate-stage prostate cancer, and twelve weeks after the operation, he had been pronounced cancer free—which was wonderful news—but almost as soon as he'd recovered much of his stamina and gotten the verdict, he'd gone into a funk, a depression that had baffled my mother and all of us around him. She'd finally managed to cajole him into taking the trip he'd always dreamed about, starting at the lighthouses on the coast of North Carolina and working his way to the Smoky Mountains on the other side of our fair state. So far he'd made it all the way east. When he hit the Atlantic Ocean, he headed up the coast from the islands of Okracoke to Corolla on the Outer Banks, and the last I'd heard, he was heading inland toward the Great Dismal Swamp. It sounded as though he was finding his way again, both on the road *and* back to his old self. Momma had tentatively offered to go with him when she'd first suggested the trip, but he'd declared that he needed to do it alone, and I knew that she'd been a bit relieved.

"You know, I've been doing some research online, and it turns out that depression isn't all that uncommon after going through everything he's faced over the course of the past nine months," I told her.

"I'm truly touched, Suzanne," Momma said, caressing my cheek briefly. "It means a great deal to me that you've come to care for my husband."

"What can I say? He's grown on me," I answered with a smile. "I have an idea. How about lunch? I can go home and grab a quick shower, and then we can go out, my treat."

"Actually, I need to speak with your husband," Momma said, a thundercloud crossing her brow. "I went by the cottage a few minutes ago, but he wasn't there. Do you have any idea when he'll be back?"

"I'm guessing two or three weeks," I said. "He got a call from a small sheriff's department in Virginia to help out on a case that's giving them fits. It's his first real consulting job, and he's really excited about it."

"Oh," Momma said. "I see."

"Is there anything *I* can help you with?" I asked. I wasn't sure what she needed, but if there was anything I could do, I'd move heaven and earth to make it happen. My mother was more than just my Momma; she was one of my best friends.

After a moment's hesitation, she said, "I'm not sure. It's probably nothing. Honestly, I shouldn't even be bothering you with it."

She started to move away when I stepped in front of her, barring her exit. "Momma, you can talk to me."

My mother seemed to consider it for a few moments, and then she reached into her oversized purse, pulled out a sheet of paper, and showed it to me. I put the deposit, my keys, and the box of donuts down on one of the outdoor tables my customers at Donut Hearts sometimes used in nicer weather to enjoy their treats and took the note from her.

Printed on it in a basic computer font, it said,

"I know what you did, and you aren't going to get away with it."

"What does it mean?" I asked her after I'd studied it for a few moments.

"Truthfully, I have no idea," she said. "I was walking out my front door this morning when I found this taped to the doorbell."

"So who exactly have you crossed *lately*?" I asked her.

"Suzanne, it's probably just a prank. I showed it to Chief Grant earlier, and that was what he thought."

"So what you're saying is that you were concerned about it enough to show it to our chief of police," I said.

Momma waved a hand in the air as though she was shooing away a pesky gnat. "I didn't go out in search of the man; I happened to see him at City Hall. I was there getting a permit for a construction project on a property I just bought when he held the door open for me. I showed him the note, and he instantly made me feel better about it. He told me that there's been a rash of pranks going on all over town and that I shouldn't worry about it."

"Good for him," I said. "But even after you spoke with Chief Grant, you still wanted to talk to Jake about it, so as far as I'm concerned, it's serious enough to look into, even if the police don't think so." I pulled out my cell phone and speed-dialed a number.

"Exactly whom are you calling?" she asked me. "Suzanne, don't bother the police chief with this again. He's got his hands full at the moment."

"As a matter of fact, I wasn't calling him," I said. "Hey, it's me," I answered when Grace Gauge, my best friend and my usual partner in my amateur investigations, answered. "Are you in town? And if so, do you have any plans this afternoon?"

"Just some dreary reports I have to fill out," she admitted. "I'd give anything to ignore them for a while. What's going on?"

"Someone left a threatening note on Momma's front door this morning. Care to help me dig into it?"

"Absolutely. Are you still at the shop?" Grace asked without hesitation.

"As a matter of fact, we're standing right in front of it even as we speak," I said.

"Don't move. I'll be right there," she answered.

Before Grace could hang up, I looked around and noticed that a few folks were out enjoying the cool weather. It had been a long, hot summer, and we were finally starting to see some chilly temperatures again. The problem was that we'd attracted their attention, and I really didn't want to discuss anything like this on the sidewalk. "Hang on. Meet us at my place instead," I said.

"I'll be there before you are," Grace said.

After I ended the call, Momma said, "Suzanne, you really shouldn't make a fuss about this."

"Listen, *nobody* gets away with threatening my mother, so with or without your cooperation, Grace and I are going to look into this. Now, we can stand here arguing about it all afternoon, or you can go ahead and give in now. Either way, it's happening, but it will be a whole lot easier with your help."

"Fine. I give up," she said with a sigh, and then allowed herself a slight grin. "How did you ever get to be so stubborn?"

"What can I say? I came by it naturally," I said. "Where's your car?"

"It's still parked in the lot at City Hall," she admitted. "I thought it would be easier just to walk over to your cottage and then here."

"Okay, it's safe enough there for the moment. Let's take the Jeep and go meet Grace back at my place."

Momma ordinarily wasn't a big fan of riding around town in my vehicle, but she got in without comment. That alone told me that the note she'd received that morning was making her more nervous than she was willing to admit.

"Dot, are you okay?" Grace asked my mother the second we walked up onto my porch to meet her.

"I'm fine, dear. I'm afraid Suzanne is overreacting."

"Let me see the note," she said, ignoring my mother's protests.

Momma handed it to her, and I thought briefly about sealing it in one of Jake's evidence bags, but it already had at least three sets of prints on it, and besides, I didn't have the means to get fingerprints off of a document, let alone compare what I found with anyone else. That was a job for the police, and evidently Chief Grant wasn't taking it too seriously.

"I know what you did, and you aren't going to get away with it."

"What exactly does that mean?" Grace asked. "We need to call Stephen."

"I've already spoken with him about it, and he believes that it's just a prank," Momma replied.

"We'll see about that," Grace said with a frown. She'd been dating our chief of police for quite a while now, and I didn't envy the scolding he was about to get from her. My mother and I were the closest things to family Grace had left in the world, and she protected Momma nearly as fiercely as I did.

Grace stepped away from us and started pacing in the open area of lawn on the brink of the park. I could hear bits and bursts of the conversation from her end, and then she rejoined us, looking frustrated. "He says this kind of thing has been happening like crazy around town over the past few days," Grace said. "He believes that some bored teenagers are playing pranks on random people and trying to shake them up a little to see how they'll react. Apparently someone left a note for Ivy Cruickshank this morning, telling her that her cat was on the roof of the bank. Ivy couldn't find Sprinkles in the yard where she usually hangs out, and she was in a panic until one of Stephen's deputies found her lazily sunning herself on the back porch; the cat, not Ivy. It was pretty clear the feline in question had never been anywhere near the bank today. There have been a handful of other notes left all over town as well, and yesterday someone took the scarecrow out of the community garden and planted it in front of Cutnip. Apparently there was a sign around its neck printed kind of like the one you got, Dot."

"What did it say?" I asked.

"*Cutnip Did This To Me!*" she answered. "There was a crude drawing of a scarecrow getting a haircut below the message. Anyway, Stephen thinks the note you got was just one more prank that some kid mistakenly thought was funny, Dot."

"This is more serious than a cat that's not missing, a few random threats, and a relocated scarecrow," I said as we all walked inside.

"That's what I just told Stephen, but he said that he was up to his elbows in real crimes at the moment, and he couldn't do anything about people pranking each other until he catches the culprit red-handed, which he is sure is going to happen sooner rather than later," she answered.

"Okay then, that just means that we'll have to do this ourselves," I said. "Momma," I asked as I led the women into the kitchen, where we took our seats at the table, "who do you know that might want to threaten you with something like this?"

"Suzanne, I can't do what I do and not ruffle a *few* feathers," she said. "At any given time, there are probably a *handful* of folks around April Springs who would like to put a scare in me."

"Okay, I get that. You're a big mover and shaker in town. Who have you aggravated *recently*, though?"

Momma thought about my question for a few moments and then said, "This is nonsense. I never should have mentioned it in the first place."

"Maybe not, but it's too late now," I said firmly.

"Please, Dot, do it for us," Grace pled. "If anything happened to you and Suzanne and I just stood by and did nothing, neither one of us would ever be able to forgive ourselves."

Momma took that in, and I realized that Grace had played the situation perfectly. *That* was the way to appeal to my mother, not through logic but emotion, especially since it involved the two of us.

"Very well. Would you like to write this down?"

"Is it honestly *that* big a list?" I asked as I reached behind me and pulled out one of Jake's notebooks and pens. He'd gotten in the habit of leaving them everywhere, basic tools he'd used quite often before he'd retired as a State Police investigator.

"Let's see," she said. "I suppose the first person we need to speak with is Gerard Mince."

"Hang on a second. The three of us need to get something straight right out of the gate. *You're* not going to play an active part in this investigation. If Grace and I are going to be able to get anyone to speak with us, it's going to have to be without you being there, too."

"That's ridiculous," Momma said dismissively. "Suzanne, I *know* these people."

"That's the reason we have to do this *without* you, Dot," Grace said calmly.

"I suppose you're right, though I don't care for it," Momma replied after a moment of hesitation.

I started to protest that I'd just told my mother basically the same thing, but I kept my mouth shut. Getting her to agree to the ground rules was more important than which one of us had made the suggestion.

At least that was what I tried to tell myself.

"Why Mr. Mince?" I asked as I jotted his name down on the first page of the notebook.

Momma smiled wryly as she said, "That construction project I mentioned that I was getting a permit for was on a building on the outskirts of town that he thought *he* had wrapped up. I happened to learn that the seller wasn't happy with the deal and was going to back out anyway, so I sweetened the offer, and he jumped at the chance to sell it to me and not Gerard. I keep telling him that if he wants to do business in April Springs, he needs to establish a presence here and not keep his head buried in Maple Hollow all of the time. The prices are quite a bit cheaper there though, and he won't budge. It's his own fault, as far as I'm concerned."

"Was that entirely legal, what you did?" I asked her gently. I knew that my mother was a mover and shaker in local real estate and also owned pieces of several businesses in the area, but I never thought she'd do anything outside of the law.

"It was all perfectly aboveboard. The seller had the option to pull out of the deal up to twenty-four hours before the sale was finalized. He exercised his option forty-five minutes before the deadline and called me."

"How did the seller happen to know you were interested in the first place?" I asked her.

"I may have mentioned something to his wife to that effect at the garden club earlier that day," Momma admitted. "I do it all of the time,

Suzanne. Honestly, if I'd known the man in question was selling that particular property, I would have paid even more for it than I did."

"So Gerard was upset with you," I said. "How angry was he?"

Momma shrugged. "Well, all I can say is that he wasn't happy. It was the third deal I've beaten him out of this year. If I had to guess, I'd say that he's fairly miffed with me at the moment."

"Enough to threaten you with a note like that?" Grace asked her.

"I suppose so, but I don't think he'd actually *do* anything," Momma said thoughtfully.

"You hesitated a bit before you said that," I stated. I knew my mother better than anyone else alive, including her husband. At least I liked to believe that was true.

Momma explained, "There have been rumors circulating for years that Gerard has done some shady things in the past, and that he's been associated with people who might not hesitate to *discourage* their competition, if you follow me. Gerard has a clean reputation now, but the stories about him when he started out are a bit chilling."

"Then he goes to the head of our list," I said. "Who else do we need to speak with?"

"Suzanne, I don't relish the thought of you and Grace doing this unchaperoned," Momma said.

"Mother, you know better than anyone that we can take care of ourselves," I answered.

"Besides, we won't put ourselves in any compromising positions," Grace assured her with more conviction than I liked.

"At least not if we can help it," I quickly added. "Who's next?"

"I suppose if you're going to speak with Gerard, you should talk to Cordelia Bush as well."

"Why Mrs. Bush?" I asked. I knew her, though slightly, and I was surprised my mother mentioned her name.

"As of late, she's been going around talking about trying to get into real estate speculation," Momma said. "She and Gerard were partners on the deal I just closed instead, and I shouldn't have to tell you about Cordelia's temper."

"No, I've seen it firsthand myself," I said. We'd made a simple mistake at Donut Hearts, or so she said, on a to-go order a few months earlier. Cordelia had acted as though it were the end of the world getting two custard-filled donuts instead of ones loaded with whipped cream. I offered her two replacements on the house, but she'd insisted on a full refund for her entire order. After arguing with her for a few minutes, I'd found it simpler to acquiesce, but after that, I made her write down her orders herself before I'd fill them, and she finally stopped coming in altogether, which was no great loss, in my opinion. "She goes on our list. Anyone else?"

"Not business related," Momma said with a frown.

"There's nothing in that note that says that this has to be about business," I told her.

"Well, I suppose you should speak with Francis Gray, then," she admitted a little reluctantly.

"Your *neighbor*?" I asked her.

"Yes, I'm afraid so. She had a tree removed that was clearly on our property in order to get a better view out of her bedroom window, and I protested vigorously. Most folks in town are afraid to stand up to her, but she made a mistake when she assumed that I was anything like most folks."

"What did you do?" I asked her, wondering just how my mother would react to such an incursion on her private property.

"I told her that I demanded financial restitution for the full value of the tree, or she had to have one replanted that equaled the size of the one she'd had removed," Momma said.

"How did she react to that?" Grace asked. "Did she refuse your demands?"

Momma grinned. "Oh, she did more than refuse. She got pretty salty with me, so I told her that if she hasn't made some kind of restitution by midnight tonight, I would see her in court. I'll do it, too."

"So, Francis could have left that note herself," I said, making a note of it.

"I doubt the woman is savvy enough to turn *on* a computer, let alone print out a threatening note," Momma said grimly.

"Nonetheless, we'll look into it," I said. I pushed the notebook aside. "Is that it?"

"Yes," she said, and then took a breath. "I believe so," she repeated.

"Who *else* should go on our list, Momma?" I asked her.

"Dot, we really do need to know," Grace added.

"It's ridiculous. There is no way Ellie Westmore would do such a thing."

"*Mrs. Westmore?*" I asked. She had been my third-grade teacher in elementary school, and while I wouldn't say that she was beloved, she'd usually had a kind word for most of the children she'd taught. "What about her?"

"She's been smitten with Phillip for years, and lately, she's become a bit too aggressive about it for my taste."

It was hard to imagine my prim and proper former teacher going after my stepfather. "Are you sure about that?"

"Suzanne, she has always had a crush on him, despite being married to Homer Westmore for forty-two years. When Homer died last month, she tried to turn to Phillip for comfort. He did his best to console her, but when she started to misread his intentions, he walked away. She hasn't given up, though."

"Why did I not know about that?" I asked her.

"Young lady, as hard as it may be for you to believe, we don't feel obligated to share *every* aspect of our lives with you all of the time."

"Where were *you* when this consoling was going on?" I asked her, refusing to rise to the bait.

"I was busy," she admitted. "By the time I knew what was happening, it was already over. Phillip was baffled that his intentions were so misconstrued, and I'm afraid that I had to have a rather stern talk with Ellie to drive the point home."

"Then it stands to reason that she might want to see you out of the picture so she can have Phillip for herself," I said, as hard as it was for me to believe. "How exactly did Homer die, anyway?" I asked idly. I'd heard that he'd passed away a few days after it had happened, but since we didn't run in the same circles and he wasn't a customer of mine, I hadn't paid all that much attention to it.

"I'm not sure that I ever heard the final official verdict, though I've heard rumors that it was supposedly a heart attack," Momma said a bit cryptically.

"Supposedly?" I asked her pointedly.

"Well, he *was* a stern man who got more severe with her with each passing year. Before she made a pass at my husband, I had a great deal of sympathy for her, so I wouldn't necessarily rule out foul play, though I have no idea what the police think."

"Are there any *other* names you'd like to add to our list?" I asked her a bit wearily.

"Isn't that enough?" Momma shook her head. "No, I'm certain that's all."

"It will give us some solid leads to follow up on," I said as I flipped the notebook closed. "Don't worry, Momma. We'll take care of this."

"Suzanne, Grace, I appreciate you both doing this, but tread softly. I don't want to upset these people if I can help it. I have to live here, you know."

"That's the beauty of it," I said. "*We'll* be the ones asking questions. In the meantime, I think you should come stay here with me while Phillip's away."

She looked shocked by the very suggestion. "I beg your pardon?"

"Momma, be reasonable. You're rattling around in that house all by yourself, and I'm doing the same thing here with Jake gone. Why don't we rattle around together?"

"Suzanne, don't be ridiculous," she said as she stood. "I'm going home."

I could see that her mind was made up, at least for the moment. "If that's the way you feel about it, at least let me give you a ride back to your car," I said as I stood as well.

"My vehicle isn't that far away," she said stiffly. "I'm perfectly capable of walking. We will speak again later."

"Dot, we're just trying to help," Grace said gently.

Momma softened instantly at Grace's words. "I know you are, dear. I'll tell you what. Let's all have dinner together tonight. Unless you have plans, that is."

I was about to tell her that I was as free as a butterfly, but Grace spoke up before I could say a word. "No, Stephen is going to be on a stakeout somewhere tonight trying to catch a bad guy, so I don't have any plans."

"I'm available too, just in case anyone cares," I added, my desire to be a smart aleck overwhelming my need to get along with my mother.

"Then you two must come over to my place at six," Momma said. She touched Grace's cheek lightly, and then she gave mine a peck. "Be careful, ladies."

"We always are," I said. I thought about following her back to her car, but I knew that she'd never stand for it.

Besides, no one would dare attack my mother in broad daylight. Would they?

Chapter 2

"SO, SHOULD WE HEAD to Maple Hollow first or stay in town?" Grace asked me.

"I'd like to speak with the folks here first," I said as I grabbed my keys. "Let's hurry, though."

"What's the rush?" Grace asked as she followed me out of the cottage.

"I want to get to Momma's place before she does," I said.

"Was there something else you needed to speak with her about?"

"No, but I want to get to Francis Gray before my mother decides to ignore our advice and confront her before we get a chance to have a little chat with her ourselves."

"Would your mother really do that?" Grace asked me as we got into my Jeep and started out of the driveway. "Strike that. Of course she would."

"I'm not saying that I would blame her," I said. "I know in the past how it's felt to feel threatened, and I didn't like it then any more than she does now."

"I knew Francis could be difficult, but would she really threaten your mother over a tree?"

"Honestly, it wasn't much of a threat, as threats go," I answered as I raced to Momma's so we could speak with her neighbor first.

"I don't know. *I know what you did, and you aren't going to get away with it* sounds a little like a threat to me."

"That's why we're tracking it down, but you have to admit that it could have been a lot worse. It might have been an outright death threat," I said.

"Do you think that's the reason Stephen wasn't any more upset about it than he appeared to be?" Grace asked me. "I was honestly surprised he didn't take it more seriously than he did."

"There's probably a good chance that he's right and that this was just one prank among many. We both know that there's a difference with this one, though," I said as I pulled up into Francis's driveway and parked.

"It was against your mother," Grace said firmly.

"That's it," I answered.

Francis Gray's house, a sweet little Cape Cod, was painted a dark shade of gray, with lighter gray shutters and a deep-gray, almost black front door and roof. It was neat, the lawn well cared for, and there were obvious signs that a tree had recently been removed from the side of the property toward the cottage Momma shared with Phillip. I could see that the landscapers had left a few gouges in the grass, and there was evidence that after the tree had been removed, Francis had paid to have the stump ground down below the surface as well. The wood chips on the ground still smelled faintly of oak, and I mourned the loss of such a lovely tree, taken down for no other reason than it had obstructed a woman's view of the distant mountains. I couldn't blame Momma for being upset about it, especially since the tree had been hers to begin with.

"Suzanne, let's remember to keep our cool when we speak with her," Grace said carefully as she studied my face.

"I'll be civil," I said as I reached for the doorbell.

Grace put a hand on mine. "Do you promise?"

"What? I'll be good," I insisted.

"Maybe, but I saw the way you were just looking at the spot where that tree was taken down," Grace cajoled me. "We're here about the threat against your mother, not the tree removal. We both know that Dot is perfectly capable of handling that part of the dispute herself."

I took a deep breath in, and then I let it out slowly. "You're right. Thanks for reminding me."

"Hey, it's a nice change of pace for *me* to be the voice of reason," Grace said with a grin. "Normally those roles are reversed."

"Well, don't get too used to it," I answered with a smile.

"Oh, I fully expect to be the one who needs to be reined in in the future," she said as she rang the bell herself.

Francis Gray came to the door dressed completely in shades of her signature namesake color. I wasn't sure that I would have done the same thing if I'd been in her shoes, but she seemed to be happy enough with the drab color scheme of her life, so who was I to judge? She'd even let her hair go gray instead of dyeing it a more youthful shade, and I saw her gray eyes studying us as she took a half step back once she knew who was visiting her. Had she been so obsessed with the color that she'd even gotten contact lenses to match? I hoped that she hadn't taken things that far, but it wouldn't have surprised me.

Francis's face clouded up the moment she saw me. "Suzanne Hart, I know why you are here. I don't care to discuss the dispute I'm having with your mother with you, so you can save your breath, young lady."

"Actually, we're here to see if you know anything about the threatening note my mother got this morning," I said as sweetly as I could manage.

The older woman looked surprised by my question. "I'm sure I don't know what you're talking about."

"Come on, Francis. You were upset with Momma. I understand that. But leaving that note was taking things a little too far, don't you think?"

She clearly looked flustered. "Not that it matters to me one bit, but I honestly don't have a clue in the world what you're talking about."

"Let me remind you. *'I know what you did, and you aren't going to get away with it.'* Ring any bells?"

"I can assure you that I never wrote any such note. The base of that tree was clearly on my property, and it was a danger that I had to take care of. The trunk was rotten, and I was concerned that it was going to fall and hit my house."

"Funny, but it had to be tough knowing one way or the other if it was rotten or not while it was still standing," I said as I glanced in the direction where the tree once stood so recently. "In fact, I can't even say for sure exactly where it was located, now that the stump and some of the roots have been ground up. It's all just one big mess. You didn't happen to take any pictures of the damaged trunk, or even the tree's original location before you had it removed, did you?"

"Now why didn't I think of that?" she asked with a wicked little smile. "I'm afraid I didn't even consider documenting what the tree removal experts found."

"That's okay. We'll just go speak with them ourselves," I said. I knew full well that I'd just told Grace that I understood that we were there about the threat and not the tree, but I couldn't just stand idly by and let Francis Gray get away with such wanton destruction, either.

"Be my guest. Go ahead and call them," she said smugly, and I knew instantly that it would be a waste of time. I was certain that she'd either bribed or threatened the crew into silence, perhaps a combination of the two, and I had a feeling that Momma wasn't going to win this particular dispute, not that it would stop her from pursuing it anyway.

"Now, about the note," Grace said, taking advantage of the fact that I was mulling over what to say next and filling the silence herself.

"What about it?" Francis asked frostily.

"Did you print it out and tape it to her door this morning or not?" I asked.

"Why would you entertain the notion for one second that I would do such a thing? It sounds more like a note your mother might leave me, not vice versa. She's under the delusion that my tree was on her property. Well, let her try to prove it now." Francis frowned for a moment before adding, "I don't have time to stand around listening to you two try your best to sully my good name. I'll thank you both to leave."

As Francis said it, she closed the door on us. It wasn't quite a slam, but it was emphatic enough.

Clearly our interview was over.

As Grace and I walked back to the Jeep, she said softly, "You know, I hate to admit it, but she's got a point. If that note had said, 'Sue me at your own risk,' I might have believed it, but the threat doesn't make sense when you think about it possibly coming from her."

"You're right," I said. "But is it wrong of me to have *wanted* it to be from her?" I asked Grace with a slight smile.

"You can't get arrested for *thinking* something," she replied with a gentle grin of her own. "Thank goodness for that, too. If that were the case, I'd be locked up for so long that I'd *never* get out. Should we cross her name off our list?"

"I don't know that we have much choice. As much as I hate to admit it, Francis has a point."

"Cheer up, Suzanne," Grace said. "We've still got three more folks we can talk to."

"True. I just hope we have more luck with them than we did with Francis Gray."

"Well, on the bright side, we couldn't have much *less* luck, could we?" I asked.

"I wouldn't think so. Who's next? Should we track Cordelia down or speak with Mrs. Westmore first?"

"I'm not particularly keen on asking my third-grade teacher if she has a crush on my stepfather," I admitted.

"You do realize that we have to ask her at some point," Grace reminded me.

"True, but not immediately."

"Then let's go see if we can find Cordelia Bush," Grace said.

For a few moments, I was wondering if Cordelia was going to answer her door at all, but I finally heard someone say loudly from inside, "Hold your horses. I'm moving as fast as I can."

"She sounds like she's in a lovely mood," Grace observed before Cordelia made it to the door. "I just love a hostile suspect, don't you?"

Cordelia finally opened the door, and somehow she looked even less pleased to see us than Francis had been, if that were possible. "Seriously? I rushed to the door for the two of *you*?"

"Were you expecting someone else?" I asked her. Then I looked down. "What happened to you, Cordelia?" Her right foot was in a walking cast, and it extended halfway up her calf.

"I took a tumble coming down the stairs three days ago," she said. "I was hoping you were bringing me some food," she added glumly.

"Why, did you order something?" Grace asked her.

"No, but I have several thoughtful friends, and I was certain that at least *one* of them would be thinking of me and my dilemma," she replied.

I had to bite my tongue at that. As far as I knew, Cordelia had lots of acquaintances, but not many friends. "Sorry about that." I suddenly remembered the donuts in the back of my Jeep. "Hey, would you like some donuts from my shop?"

"What kind do you have?" she asked skeptically, as though she was doing me a favor and not vice versa.

Was she seriously going to quibble about the selection? "They're on the house, and I'm sure you'll be able to find something to your liking in the box. I'll be right back."

"That's okay, Suzanne. I'll grab them for you," Grace volunteered as she sped down the steps.

"I used to be able to move like that before I broke my ankle," Cordelia said wistfully as she watched Grace.

I doubted that she'd *ever* been able to move like my best friend did, but I kept that observation to myself. Cordelia was forty pounds past heavyset, and I was pretty sure my donuts weren't going to do her waistline any good, but at least as far as I could see, she wasn't all that intent on fighting the losing battle with her weight anyway. Still, I felt a little guilty about adding to her problems. "You don't have to eat any if you don't want them," I said lamely.

"What choice do I have? If I don't, I'll starve to death," Cordelia answered.

I sincerely doubted that, but it wouldn't have been kind of me to point it out. "How tough is it for you to get around?"

"I broke my ankle," she said testily. "What do you think?"

"I'm so sorry," I said, mustering up as much sympathy as I could manage. "You seem to have had quite a run of bad luck lately, haven't you?"

"What do you mean by that?" she asked me as her gaze narrowed.

"Well, I heard about my mother's most recent real estate transaction. You and Gerard Mince lost out on a good investment opportunity, didn't you?"

Cordelia waved a hand in the air. "I didn't care about that. The truth was that I wasn't even sure that I wanted to be a part of that deal anyway. If anything, your mother did me a favor cutting us out of it, even if she did act dirty and underhanded to get her way. She should be ashamed of herself for the way she conducts business, throwing her weight around the way she does and being so sneaky when it suits her, all the while walking around town shoving her piety in everyone's face."

"How did she do you a favor?" I asked, keeping my opinion of Cordelia's characterization of my mother to myself. I wasn't sure how long I was going to be able to bite my tongue, though. I needed my investigating partner there to keep me in check, so where was she? I glanced back at the Jeep and saw that Grace was taking her sweet time retrieving the donuts while she chatted on the phone with someone.

"I inherited some money from my mother, and in a moment of weakness, I listened to my brother-in-law in Hickory, who happens to be a financial advisor. He introduced Betty—that's my sister—and me to Gerard, telling us that we had to do something with the money or we'd be complete fools. I never thought of having extra money as being a burden until he started telling us both that we were insane to keep it all in Treasury bills. Anyway, I let them talk me into investing most of it in real estate, but your mother saved me from my folly. I fired my brother-in-law as soon as the deal fell through, at least as my financial advisor, though I wish I could fire him from being Betty's husband, too."

"Was Gerard Mince as pleased as you were when the deal fell through?" I asked her.

"I should say not! I thought he was going to have a coronary on the spot! He swore he'd get even with your mother if it was the last thing he ever did." Pausing a moment, she added, "She'd better watch her back around him. He's looking for blood."

Grace rejoined us with donuts in hand. "Sorry about that. I had to take a call," she said as she extended the box toward Cordelia.

I grabbed it instead and flipped it open to show her the contents. "Do you see any you like in particular?"

Both women looked at me oddly, equally puzzled by my actions, but I had a reason for my behavior.

"Are you telling me that they're not *all* for me?" Cordelia asked me sullenly.

"Sorry, but I promised some to a few other folks as well," I lied.

"Could I at least have two?" she asked me, the whine heavy in her voice.

"Absolutely," I said. "But only two, I'm afraid."

Without hesitation, she chose the lone bear claw and an oversized cinnamon roll, the two biggest treats in the box. "Thank you," she said a little wistfully as she looked at the rest of the goodies as I closed the lid quickly before she could make a grab for something else.

"You're very welcome," I said as sweetly as I could manage. I'd throw the rest of the donuts in the dumpster before I'd give them to her after her comments about my mother. Cordelia was going to have to pay a jerk tax for that crack, in the form of losing out on a handful of other treats. Maybe in the future she'd speak a little nicer about my mother, but I doubted it. "Feel better."

"As though that were even possible," Cordelia said as she struggled with the door. With her hands full of treats and one leg in a cast, it wasn't exactly easy for her.

Grace started to offer to help her, but I shook my head, and instead we walked back to my Jeep and got in. I stowed the remaining donuts on the floor behind Grace's seat and then turned to face my friend, who was studying me calmly.

"What was that about?" Grace asked. "I thought they were *all* for her." After I relayed what she'd said about Momma, she added, "Given what she said, I'm surprised you gave her *any*."

"I couldn't quite be that heartless, but the rest might come in handy with our other two suspects. I can't believe that Cordelia was a dud, too."

"Why, do you honestly believe her story about being *happy* the deal fell through?" Grace asked me as we drove away.

"As a matter of fact, I do, but even if I didn't, could you see her tottering up to Momma's place, taping that note onto the doorbell, and then hustling away before anyone saw her?"

"No, that's a fair point. With that cast, she would have been easy to spot, and her getaway wouldn't be more than a slow escape. I guess that means we're zero for two. Suzanne, I know you're not happy about the prospect, but we have to bite the bullet and go talk to Mrs. Westmore next, unless you want to drive to Maple Hollow instead."

"No, let's go have an unpleasant conversation with my former teacher before we do that. By the way, who was that on the phone?"

"I'll tell you at lunch," Grace said. "You *were* planning on feeding me something other than day-old donuts, weren't you?"

"If the Boxcar Grill is okay with you, let's go right now," I said, trying to at least put off the next interview that I wasn't all that eager to be a part of.

"It sounds wonderful to me," she replied.

Maybe I *was* just delaying the conversation I didn't want to have with my former teacher, but I was hungry too, and a visit with Trish Granger, the owner of the diner, was always a welcome diversion.

After all, we still had to eat, didn't we?

Chapter 3

WE NEVER MADE INTO the diner though, at least not right away. Emily Hargraves—owner of the Two Cows and a Moose newsstand and perennially engaged to my ex-husband, Max—approached us the moment we got out of my Jeep. "Suzanne, you haven't seen Max, have you?"

"Not for a few weeks," I admitted. "Why, is he looking for me? What's going on?"

Emily clouded up. "He needs to speak with you."

I was getting a bit concerned now. "Emily, if there's something I should know, I'd love it if you'd tell me yourself. I hate surprises, and now that I know there's something on Max's mind, you'd be doing me a favor by telling me yourself."

"I suppose I can see that," she said, and then bit her lip. "May we speak in private?"

"I'll go grab us a table," Grace said, but I put a hand on her arm.

"It's okay," I told her as I turned to Emily. "You can say anything you need to tell me in front of Grace."

"I don't mind, Suzanne," Grace insisted.

"Stay," I told her, and then I gave Emily a brighter smile than I felt at the moment. "Go on. What is it?"

"Max and I got married yesterday," Emily said, searching my expression for some kind of reaction. "We eloped."

Chapter 4

AFTER THE BRIEFEST of pauses, I hugged my friend. "Congratulations," I said with as much enthusiasm as I could muster. I knew they'd been trying to plan their wedding again after the first attempt failed so miserably, but I hadn't realized they might elope.

"*He* was supposed to be the one to tell you, but I can't find him anywhere," Emily said.

"You might want to invest in one of those tracking devices they use on pets," Grace said with a smile. Her grin took a bit of the sting out of her comment, but it was clear that she was worried about me, even though she and Emily were friends as well.

"I've considered it," the new bride said with a faint grin. "Suzanne, you're part of the reason, you know."

"Are you saying that you married him because of *me*?" I asked, suddenly taken aback.

"You vouched for him, and I saw that you were right. He's a changed man."

"I'm sincerely happy for you," I said as I got used to the idea that my ex-husband was remarried, "and I wish you nothing but happiness."

Emily grinned again, and I saw that she was weeping slightly as she hugged me fiercely. "I *told* him that you'd be happy for us, but he was afraid to tell you himself."

"No worries, Emily. Max and I buried the hatchet a long time ago," I said, and it was true. We'd formed some kind of odd friendship in the years since he'd cheated on me and I'd divorced him, as much as that defied logic in some folks' opinions around town. "Tell him not to sweat it, okay?"

"I will if I can ever find him," she said as she left us and headed down Springs Drive toward the hardware store, no doubt in search of her errant spouse.

"Suzanne, are you okay?" Grace asked me as we started up the steps. "I'm fine," I said.

"Is that the truth?" she asked, holding my arm gently back before I could go inside.

"If I hadn't found Jake, it might be a different story. When I found out that Max had cheated on me, it wrecked my world, but I found the love of my life, and that helped take a lot of the anger out of it for me. It's pretty clear that he loves Emily in a way that he could never love me, and I'm fine with that. I wonder why he didn't tell me himself, though. It's not like he didn't know where to find me. I'm at Donut Hearts most mornings."

"I'm sure it was because the coward didn't have the nerve," Grace said. Before I could protest, she held up a hand. "I know *you've* put it behind you, but I'm still holding onto a bit of a grudge after what he did to you."

"As far as I'm concerned, it's all water over the bridge now," I said, grinning at her, purposely mangling the old saying to get a smile from her. "Thanks for being my best friend. You've always had my interests at heart. It's something I've counted on more times than I can tell you, and you helped me over the roughest patch I've been through in my life, at least so far."

"You've done the same thing for me," Grace said as she released my arm.

"Then it's a good thing that we've got each other. Now let's eat. I'm starving."

"At least your appetite is still good," she said with a bit of a laugh.

"If that ever goes away, *then* you'll know that I've got problems," I answered in kind.

"Have you heard the news?" Trish asked me the second we walked into the Boxcar Grill.

"Yes, we know Max and Emily eloped," I said. "I'm fine."

"What? They eloped? When did that happen?" Trish was clearly surprised to hear the news I'd just spilled.

"You didn't know? What are you talking about?"

"I knew that Max had disappeared, but I didn't know that he and Emily *eloped*. Are you okay, Suzanne?"

"Truthfully, I'm a little hungry, but besides that, I'm perfectly all right," I said, wondering how many times I'd have to reassure folks that I was okay as soon as they heard the news. I hadn't meant to spill the beans about Emily. "Don't tell anyone until they announce it themselves, okay?"

She shrugged as she pointed to the dining room, where fifteen of her diners were hanging on every word. "I won't, but I can't speak for any of them."

I thought about pleading to them for their silence, but I knew it was futile. It couldn't be undone, and I realized that I'd just revealed a secret that hadn't been mine to share.

There was only one thing that I could do, so I grabbed my phone and called Emily Hargraves.

"Listen, I figured that you already told Trish about eloping with Max, but I spilled the beans. I'm so sorry."

"It's okay," Emily said with a laugh. "We were going to start telling people as soon as Max spoke with you. That's why I was so eager to find you."

"I get that, but I still should have kept my mouth shut," I said, apologizing again.

"Don't give it another thought," she said happily. "I'm just glad I don't have to keep it a secret anymore."

"Was she upset?" Grace asked me when I hung up.

"No, she acted as though I did her a favor," I admitted.

"Then all's well that ends well," Grace said. "Let's eat."

"Max is still missing," I reminded her.

"He's probably just hiding somewhere until the coast is clear," Grace replied. "Anyway, it's not our monkeys, and it's not our circus."

It was an expression we'd picked up lately concerning things that were none of our business, and we were both enjoying it way too much. "You're right," I said.

Trish smiled and asked, "Why don't you two sit up here by me? I haven't seen you both in ages, and I'd love to catch up."

"Sounds good," I said as we took the table by the register and closest to the door into the kitchen. As far as I was concerned, it was prime real estate, and I was happy it was free.

After we'd ordered a pair of lunch specials—white chicken chili and cornbread, with sweet iced tea—Trish asked us, "What do you think about what's going on around town?"

"What do you mean?" I asked her.

"Apparently some kids are leaving notes everywhere trying to rile folks up. Don't tell me you didn't get one at the cottage."

"No, but Momma got one," I admitted. "Have there really been that many of them?" Were we chasing shadows trying to find out if anyone had a vendetta against my mother after all?

"I got one here at the Boxcar," she admitted. "At least four customers have gotten them, too. They even stole the scarecrow from the community garden and put it in front of Cutnip."

"We heard about that," I admitted. "What did your note say?" I was hoping that it mimicked the one Momma had received. Then I would know that it hadn't been personal.

"It said, *'What's really in your meatloaf? If you don't tell the world, we're going to!'* Like I'd ever use anything but top-grade sirloin. Hilda would skin me alive if I ever tried to use anything else. You know how she feels about her meatloaf."

"Were the other notes so specific?" Grace asked. It was an excellent question, because Momma's had sounded a bit generic to me.

"All of the ones I've heard about so far were," she said.

"Would you mind if we saw the note you got?" I asked. I wanted to compare the font as well as the paper they'd used.

"I threw it away," she said, frowning. "What exactly did your mother's note say, Suzanne?"

"It said, *I know what you did, and you aren't going to get away with it.* That doesn't sound like the ones everyone else has been getting."

"Yeah, I see your point. Hang on a second." She disappeared in back, and after a few minutes, Trish came out with a piece of paper housed in a baggy.

"Were you trying to protect any fingerprints on it?" I asked her as I took it from her.

"No, I just didn't want you to have to handle it directly, since it was in my trash can," she admitted.

I looked at the note, and I knew in an instant that the threat that had been left for my mother was quite different from the one that Trish had received. Not only was the font different, but it was clearly a cheaper grade of paper. "Do you mind if I keep this?" I asked her.

"I don't care. Just don't show it around town. You know how easily rumors get started around here."

"I'll keep it under wraps," I said. "Do you have any idea who else got notes?"

"Let's see. So far there's the hardware store, the bookstore, and Ivy Cruickshank," she said. "Ivy's was about her cat. That's the only one I actually saw besides the one at Cutnip."

"Was it like yours?" I asked her.

"It looked just like it," she admitted, "but that was before I saw the one they put in my mailbox, so I couldn't say for sure."

"Hang on. It wasn't taped to your front door?" I asked her.

"No, it was in the box. Why?"

"Just collecting information," I said. "Thanks. You've been a huge help."

"I don't see how, but you're welcome. Your food should be ready, since Hilda just has to scoop it out of a big pot, and we're offering a new white/wheat bread I'm making myself while supplies last, if you'd like that instead of cornbread."

"That sounds perfect! I'm glad we got here in time for that," I said with a smile.

"I've been on a real bread-making kick lately," Trish admitted. "It's amazing what all you can do with such simple ingredients."

"Having the knowhow helps," I reminded her. "I do the same thing myself."

"Hey, I'm not treading on your toes offering fresh bread, am I?" she asked, clearly concerned about the possibility of stealing some of my customers away from me.

"No, as long as they aren't sweet and shaped like donuts, we're good," I answered with a grin.

The grill owner nodded and headed for the kitchen. While she was gone, I turned to Grace. "You were going to tell me about that telephone call you got earlier."

"It was nothing," Grace said evasively.

"Funny, but it didn't sound like nothing to me," I said.

"Stephen told me that he needed to see me tonight," she said somberly. "I let him know that I already had dinner plans because of his stakeout, but he said that it couldn't wait." She paused a moment and then added so softly I had to strain to hear her say, "Suzanne, I think he's going to break up with me."

"Why would you say that? I didn't think you two had ever been closer."

"I thought so too, but he sounded so serious that I'm pretty sure it's not going to be good. Don't worry about it. I'll deal with whatever happens later. For now, let's focus on who had the misfortune to threaten your mother and bring on our wrath."

"Grace, you know that I'm always here for you."

"I do," she said as she touched my hand lightly. "And I may take you up on it later, but for now, I don't want to talk about it anymore, okay?"

I was still trying to decide what I could do next when Trish rejoined us with two large bowls of soup and a platter piled high with bread. "Wow, that all smells amazing," I said as I let the aromas waft toward my nose.

"It is. I've already had the chicken chili three times this week. Hilda's been perfecting the recipe, and this is the first day we're offering it on the menu. Unless I miss my guess, it's going to be a real hit around here, especially once it gets really chilly. Huh. It just occurred to me. Is that how chili got its name?"

"Beats me," I said with a shrug as I tasted the first spoonful. "Wow. That's amazing. I don't suppose I could get the recipe, could I?" The blend of shredded chicken and great northern white beans in chicken stock was incredible. There were a few spices I couldn't quite put my finger on, but the chili had clearly been enriched with what had to be sour cream and some kind of other milk product.

"I'll do even better than that," Trish said with a smile. "I'll sell you all of the soup you want, any time we have it on hand."

"But no recipe, right?" I asked with a smile.

"Suzanne, if Hilda taught you how to make it, we wouldn't see you around here nearly as much as we're about to," she replied with a laugh. "I should warn you though, the stuff's addicting."

"I've already figured that out," I replied as I dipped some of the crusty artisanal bread into the soup bowl. "Outstanding."

"The chili, or the bread?" she asked, watching me carefully.

"Both," I answered quickly.

"I can live with that," she said as Betsy Wilkes approached to pay for her meal. Betsy was a petite older woman around my mother's age, and it was clear they went to the same hairdresser, since their hairstyles were identical. In deference to the chilly air we were experiencing, she was wearing a mid-length bold red-and-black plaid jacket.

"Take your time, Trish," Betsy said with a smile. "Ladies, how are you?"

"We're well," Grace said. "How about you?"

"If I were any better, I'd have to spit," Betsy answered with a grin. Betsy was known for her odd expressions that puzzled most of us, but she was nearly always happy, and that compelled the rest of us to cut her some slack when it came to her lingo. "Did you see the scarecrow this morning?"

"We did," I answered. "You didn't happen to see who did it, did you?"

"No, ma'am, but I did see *something* a bit odd this morning over at your mother's place."

"What's that?" I asked.

"I was out for my early-morning walk before sunup, just like I do every day, and I could swear I saw someone leaving your mother's porch and running around the back of the house a little after six a.m. Chief Martin's gone at the moment, isn't he?"

"He is," I admitted. "Did you happen to see who it might have been?"

"No, but whoever it was must have just taped something on your mother's door. I thought it was odd at the time, and then with all of these notes turning up around April Springs, I figured I'd better mention it to her. I couldn't say if the culprit were young or old, but whoever it was surely wasn't afraid of making tracks out of there the second they spotted me. I had on my headlight, you know. It's built right into my hat, and I use it more so folks can see me in the dark rather than vice versa. Anyway, I've already stopped by your mother's place once to tell her what I saw, but she was out, so I was on my way over there this very minute to try again. If you'll tell her for me, you'll save me a trip, and I have to get back home before my dog's bladder busts. Old Sal is getting on in years, and if he doesn't get his afternoon walk in time, we're both unhappy about it, if you know what I mean. That dog starts tap-dancing like a spider on ice if I'm more than a few minutes late."

"I'll let her know," I said. "Thanks for telling me."

"I'm just sorry I couldn't share anything more helpful," Betsy said.

"Don't sell yourself short," I said. "I appreciate you looking out for Momma, and the rest of the town, in the wee hours of the morning."

"That's me, a one-woman patrol," she said with a grin. "Between my morning and afternoon strolls around the neighborhood, I've got it all covered."

After Trish checked her out, the grill owner came back. I was just about finishing up my bowl, and Grace had already polished hers off completely.

"Seconds are half price," Trish said with a grin, "though I can't give you any more bread. That was the last of this batch."

"Thanks for the offer, but I'm stuffed," I said. "As tempting as it might be, if I eat any more, I won't be able to do anything but go home and take a nap."

"I can think of worse ways to spend the afternoon after going to work as early as you do, Suzanne." She turned to Grace and asked, "What about you?"

"I'm really full too, but I'll probably be back for more tomorrow," she said.

"We'll be ready for you," Trish said with a smile.

After I paid my portion of the lunch bill, knowing that Grace would protest if I picked the entire check up, Trish said, "I really am sorry to hear about Max and Emily."

"You know what? I'm not," I said. "I'm glad they found each other."

"That's sweet of you to say, Suzanne."

"I mean every word of it," I told her. "Everyone deserves a second chance at love."

"In my case, I think I'm on chance number forty-four, but that doesn't keep me from trying," she answered with a smile. "One of these days, I'm going to find my better half, and in the meantime, I'm planning on continuing to rock it solo."

"I have all the faith in the world in you," I said with a grin. "On both counts."

Chapter 5

"I SUPPOSE WE'VE PUT it off long enough," I told Grace as we got into my Jeep. "Let's go have ourselves a chat with Mrs. Westmore."

"Maybe we should start by calling her Ellie," Grace suggested. "After all, third grade was a long, long time ago."

"True, and if I use her first name, she might not be so intimidating to me," I admitted.

"Suzanne, I can't imagine *anyone* intimidating you. After all, you're one of the only people in the world who can stand up to your mother and live to tell the tale."

"Maybe so, but she's family, so she loses a bit of the fear factor for me. Mrs. Westmore, I mean Ellie, never did."

"Then maybe it's high time that she did," Grace said.

"That's easy for you to say," I told her. "You had Mr. Griswold."

"Hey, he was tough, too," she protested.

"Sure, but not Mrs. Westmore tough," I corrected her.

"True," Grace allowed. "Still, we're a pair of accomplished and successful women, Suzanne. We can do this."

"I hope you're right," I said.

"Suzy Hart, how nice to see you," Mrs. Westmore said after answering her door. She was retired from the school system, and I had no idea what she did with herself now. I couldn't imagine ever leaving Donut Hearts, even in the distant future. I'd seen what early retirement had nearly done to my husband, and I was happy that he'd finally found a purpose in life again. That wasn't to say that I thought the concept of retirement itself was bad. It was just that I knew that it was important to have a plan, whether it was volunteering, a new hobby, or traveling. The main thing was not to just sit around and wait to die, as I'd seen a few older friends do once they'd left their jobs. One of my customers in particular, a bright and jovial fellow who came into Donut Hearts every day on his way into work to buy donuts for his staff, had gleefully counted down the days until he could retire. The only problem was that after he finally pulled the trigger, he hadn't lasted six months before he passed away. He'd come in a few weeks before he died, and I noticed immediately that the spark was gone from his gaze. At least I wouldn't have to worry about that happening to Momma. She was busier now than ever, and even Phillip had thrown himself into researching cold-case crimes from long ago, a hobby that seemed to consume him at times.

"I nearly forgot that we called you that in elementary school," Grace said with a laugh.

"It was for the third grade only," I said, remembering that Mrs. Westmore had hung that nickname on me, even adapting it to "Suzy Q" for a while.

Wow, I'd forgotten how much I had hated that. "Mrs. Westmore," I said formally, and then I asked, "May I call you Ellie? It seems silly to refer to you by your last name now that I'm an adult."

She looked a bit taken aback by my forwardness, which was what I'd wanted. If she had been under the impression that I was still under her thumb, just as I'd been when I'd been a child, she was in for a surprise. "Of course, Suzanne," she said contritely.

So, my message *had* been received. I felt a bit kindlier toward her after that, and I decided to let the hint of animosity that had remained from my past go. "We're here to speak with you about my mother."

"She's all right, isn't she?" Ellie asked with a bit too much concern in her voice. It surprised me, but I found that even referring to her by her first name in my head was enough to dispel the aura of authority she'd held over me long ago.

"Oh, she couldn't be better. I understand you two had an issue not that long ago."

My former teacher frowned. "I wouldn't have expected her to share that with you."

"Why not? She's not just my mother; she's one of my best friends. Is it true that you have a crush on my stepfather?" I could have referred to Phillip by name, but I wanted to remind her that he was a part of my family and not just some random stranger.

Ellie at least had the decency to look a bit flustered. "I'm afraid the situation was misconstrued and confused from the offset."

"Then why don't you enlighten us?" Grace asked serenely.

"I'm honestly not sure what all of the fuss is about," Ellie said after biting her lower lip for a moment. "I turned to Phillip in a moment of weakness for comfort, strictly as a friend, and he misunderstood my intentions completely."

"Did Momma misunderstand, too?" I asked her, letting a hint of steel come through my voice.

"I needed someone to talk to, and to be fair, Phillip offered. I never had the slightest intention of doing anything to pursue a relationship with him, no matter what he might have believed."

I had to give her that much. Ellie wasn't backing down from her story that the fault had been with my mother and her husband, not with her.

"When's the last time you were at my mother's cottage?" I asked her.

"What? I'm not at all certain that I've *ever* been there. It's over on Mulberry Lane, isn't it?"

"No," I said curtly. "Will Momma and Phillip be able to confirm that?"

"Wait, I remember now. I brought them a fruit basket when they moved as a housewarming present. You'll have to forgive me. My memory isn't what it used to be."

I had a tough time believing that. The woman seemed as sharp as ever, and I doubted that she'd missed a single step these days. She was in her early sixties, and it was clear that she'd kept herself in shape. It was time to change tacks. "I was sorry to hear about your husband."

"Yes, it was a tragedy," she agreed, though I thought for a moment I'd seen something, a short burst of anger, flash through her look. "That was why I needed someone to lean on."

"And Phillip was the one you turned to," I said, pushing a bit harder. "It must be hard seeing your crush happy with someone else."

I knew as soon as I said it that I'd gone a bit too far, at least that quickly. Ellie tensed up, and I lost sight of the sweet woman who had once been my teacher. "As I said earlier, that's simply not true. Suzanne, I had higher expectations for the way you'd turn out than what I'm seeing demonstrated right now."

The old me would have taken her statement as a crushing blow, but I'd suffered a great many slings and arrows over the years, so all I did was smile. "Well, we can't always get what we want, but then again, look who I'm telling."

My former teacher looked as shocked by my statement as if I'd physically slapped her. Ellie didn't say another word as she stepped back into her home and closed the door in our faces.

"Wow, you let her have it with both barrels," Grace said as we walked back to my Jeep. "Remind me never to get on your bad side."

"I suddenly remembered that *she* was the one who pegged me with that Suzy Q nickname, and I got a little upset," I admitted. "Was it my imagination, or did she overreact when I said that we can't always get what we want?"

"No, you clearly struck a nerve. I was getting ready to ask her about her whereabouts this morning when you went after her. I'm guessing that being a retired teacher, she's computer literate, so printing up that threat would be easy enough for her, but I would love to know what she was up to at six when Betsy spotted someone on your mother's porch this morning."

"Sorry about that," I apologized. "We'll just have to ask her the next time we speak with her."

"Do you honestly think Ellie Westmore is going to be all that eager to talk to us again after what just happened?" Grace asked me.

"Come on. What did I say that was really all *that* bad?" I asked her as I started the Jeep and began to drive toward Maple Hollow so we could interview Gerard Mince.

"Let's see. You implied that she made a pass at your stepfather and that she harbored a secret crush for the man while her late husband was still alive. Suzanne, you did everything but accuse her of getting rid of her husband so she could be with Phillip. What did you think was going to happen?"

"Was I really *that* awful?" I asked. "I'd better apologize to her the next time we speak. In fact, maybe I should do it right now." I turned the Jeep around without waiting for Grace's approval.

"Do you honestly think she's in the mood to see us again so soon after that?" she asked me.

"Maybe not, but I've got donuts, remember? Maybe she'll accept them from me as an apology, and that might get us the chance to ask her about her morning after all."

Grace laughed. "Suzanne, I've got to hand it to you."

"Why is that?" I asked as I pulled back into the woman's driveway.

"You've got spunk," she said with a smile. "I can't wait to see if you can pull this off."

"I can't, either," I said with a shrug, "but I'm sure I'll come up with something."

"Why not? After all, who needs a plan when you're so good at ad-libbing?" she asked me.

"Let's hope it works out," I replied.

Ellie Westmore didn't want to come to the door; that much was obvious. I rang her bell for the fourth time when Grace tugged at my arm, nearly spilling the remaining donuts tucked under it. "Come on. You gave it your best shot. You could always leave them here and add a note."

"I could, but that's not going to do our investigation any good," I said, ringing the bell for what I hoped was the fifth, and lucky, try.

To my surprise, it worked. The door opened, and Ellie Westmore stood in the frame, not budging an inch. Had she been crying? I felt really bad if I'd been the cause of that. After all, it was a harmless nickname, and it had been a great many years ago. Why was I still so worked up about it? "Sorry if I got a little carried away earlier," I said. "It's just that someone left a threatening note on Momma's door this morning, and we're trying to track down its source."

"And you think it may have been me?" she asked incredulously. "You have an odd way of apologizing, Suzanne, if that is indeed what you are attempting to do."

"If you could just tell us where you were around six this morning, it would help a lot," Grace said kindly.

"I was asleep, alone, since my husband passed away, so I have no way of proving it. I'm curious, though. What exactly did the note say?"

I wasn't about to tell her if she hadn't been its author. "Do you have a computer and a printer here?" I asked, ignoring her request.

"Of course I do," she said dismissively. Then she appeared to notice the donut box under my arm. "What are those?"

"Part of my peace offering," I said as I extended them toward her.

She made no move to accept them. "Thank you, but I'm afraid I'll have to decline your kind offer."

It was my turn to be a bit flustered. I hated it when someone turned down my donuts, especially when they were free. "Are you sure?"

"I'm positive. It's not that I wouldn't enjoy them, but I find that the older I get, the more closely I have to monitor my calorie intake," she said. "Now, if you'll excuse me, I have an appointment at Cutnip in fifteen minutes. I really must go."

She brushed past us, doing her best to put on a brave smile, although it was obvious my earlier behavior had distressed her, and hurriedly walked to her car.

"Well, that didn't go too well," I said.

"Hey, at least she didn't take them and throw them in your face," Grace answered. "Besides, she didn't exactly eliminate herself from our list of suspects, and that's the first time that's happened today."

"True," I said, "though I'm not so sure the note fits her situation with Momma any more than it did with Francis."

"Maybe, but at least she's got two good legs, which puts her a step ahead of Cordelia Bush, no pun intended."

"If Cordelia's ankle is really broken, anyway," I said.

"That cast looked pretty real to me, Suzanne," Grace answered.

"Maybe I'm just being paranoid, but it all seemed a bit too convenient to me."

"Well, you know what they say. There are times when even paranoid people are right about someone being out to get them. We'll follow up and see if we can corroborate Cordelia's story about her broken ankle. In the meantime, what say we take a drive to Maple Hollow and see what Gerard Mince has to say for himself?"

"I'm game if you are," I said as I tucked the remaining donuts back into the Jeep before taking off.

Maybe we'd be able to use them again after all, and if not, I was certain that I'd be able to find *someone* to take them off my hands.

It was getting to be a point of pride with me now that they'd been rejected.

There were two vehicles parked in front of Gerard Mince's office, a cute little red sports car and a dark-blue SUV. Both hoods were cool to the touch, so they'd been there for a while. I had high hopes, but unfortunately, we were stonewalled at Gerard's office by a frosty receptionist whose dress was both too tight *and* too short. She seemed to feel that it was her life's goal not to give out any information unnecessarily. All we managed to get out of her was that her boss was not currently at the office. When he'd be back was anyone's guess, and we weren't invited to wait around for him.

"What should we do?" I asked Grace in a whisper.

"I don't see any reason to hang around here," she said, matching my volume with her own. "The ice princess certainly isn't going to tell us anything."

Evidently there wasn't anything wrong with the woman's hearing, because her glare in our direction seemed to intensify instantly, though I'd have been hard pressed to believe that it could have gotten any colder than it had been before.

"Come on," I said in my normal voice.

"Thanks for *all* of your help," Grace said to the woman sweetly. She shivered before adding, "Is it just me, or is it chilly in here?"

"It's just you," the woman said without cracking the slightest of smiles.

Once we were outside, I said, "Don't look now, but I think you've got a fan back there."

"What can I say? My charm knows no bounds. What should we do next?"

"I don't see any reason to stay in Maple Hollow, unless you want to do some shopping." The town was known for its antique shops, and I knew Grace liked to occasionally browse.

"No thanks. Let's head back," she answered.

"Okay," I said. I stopped dead in my tracks. "Grace, look at that."

"What is it?" she asked as she looked toward where I was pointing.

"The SUV is gone," I reported.

"I can't believe that weasel snuck out the back door and ran away," Grace said with a frown. "Why would he want to duck us?"

"Maybe he has something to hide," I said. "That's encouraging."

"Do you think he's the one who left that note for your mother?"

"Well, him vanishing like that certainly doesn't ease my mind about him," I admitted.

"So what do we do now?" Grace asked.

"Let's head back to April Springs. First, I'm going to give Momma a quick call though, and catch her up on what we've done so far." I pulled out my phone before I started the Jeep and found that the battery to my cell phone was completely dead. "Blast it, I forgot to charge it this morning."

"Do you want to use mine?" Grace offered as she began to dig it out of her purse.

"No, it will wait until dinner. It's not like we have anything startling to report anyway. So far we've ruled one suspect out, two more seem unlikely, and we can't find the fourth one. It appears this isn't going to be as easy as I'd hoped."

"We both know that's the way it goes sometimes," she said. "We'll figure this out, one way or the other."

"Unless it was just one more random prank after all," I said as we headed back to April Springs.

"That's the thing though, isn't it? There wasn't anything all that specific about the note your mother got, but everyone else's was tailored to the recipient. Plus, the paper was different, and so was the font. I don't think they're related at all."

"I find it hard to swallow that it was just a coincidence that the notes were all left on the same day," I said.

"But not the same way," Grace said. "The others were left in the mailboxes, while your mother's was taped to her doorbell. Could whoever have left the note for her have possibly known what was going on and then decided to take advantage of the situation to tweak your mother?"

"I suppose it's possible," I admitted. "Do me a favor. Look around in the glove box for my charger, would you?"

"I meant it when I offered you my phone," Grace said, though she complied with my request as she said it.

"Jake wouldn't know to call you, and I hate being out of touch when he's away," I admitted.

"There's nothing here, at least not a charger, anyway," Grace said after she rummaged through the glove box. "When was the last time you cleaned this thing out?"

"That all depends. What year is this?" I asked her with a grin.

"What should I do with all of this stuff?" Grace had a great deal of the flotsam and jetsam from my life sitting in her lap at that moment, odds and ends that had somehow managed to find their way there.

"Just cram it all back in, and I'll deal with it later," I told her.

"Tell me it will at least be this year," Grace said as she tried to comply with my request.

"One can always hope," I said with a grin.

We made it back to April Springs without incident, and I was driving past City Hall when the mayor himself flagged us down.

I pulled over in front of the building as Grace rolled her window down. "What's up, Mr. Mayor?" she asked him.

"Suzanne, you need to get out of the car. There's something I need to tell you." The expression on his face was completely devoid of humor—and hope as well.

"What is it, George? Did something happen to Jake?"

"No, not that I know of, at least," the mayor said. "When was the last time you spoke with your mother?"

I didn't care for that question one bit. "Less than three hours ago," I asked. "Why? What's going on?"

"Someone was struck down by a car not four houses from her doorstep ten minutes ago, and from the description I got, it could be your mother. There was some, er... damage done to her face, and they couldn't be sure of the identification."

I felt myself grow faint, but I fought to hold onto consciousness. "Where is she now?"

"On her way to the hospital," he said. "Hang on. I'll get my truck and drive you there."

"I can do it myself," I said as I jumped into the Jeep.

"Suzanne, at least let me drive," Grace offered as we sped right back in the direction we'd just come from.

"No thanks. I can handle it." I wasn't in the mood to argue the point, and she clearly realized it. I knew that Momma liked to walk sometimes in the late afternoon, especially when she was troubled by something and wanted to clear her head.

"I didn't even ask George who was driving the car that hit her," I told Grace as I raced through town. If Stephen Grant or one of his deputies wanted to give me a ticket for speeding, they were going to have to do it at the hospital, because I wasn't going to stop for anything short of a barricade.

"Does it really matter at this point?" she asked me as she pulled out her phone.

"Who are you calling?" I asked as I glanced in her direction.

"Your mother," she said. "After all, you heard George. It might not even be her."

After a full minute, Grace put her phone away.

"She didn't pick up, did she?" I asked woodenly.

"Suzanne, there could be a million reasons she didn't answer," Grace said, doing her best to comfort me.

"Really? Because right now, I can think of only one."

We got to the hospital in record time, and as I pulled into the emergency room parking area, I was racing for the door before the Jeep seemed to even come to a complete stop. The entry door banged open as I ran inside, but I didn't care.

Right now, all that mattered was that I got to Momma's side while I still had a chance to see her, maybe for the very last time.

Chapter 6

"NURSE, I NEED TO SEE the woman who was brought in here in the ambulance right now!" I shouted at the woman on duty at the front desk.

"Name, please?" she asked me officiously, not even fazed by my demeanor.

"Suzanne Hart," I said impatiently.

She tapped a few keys into her computer, and then she frowned. "I'm sorry, but I don't have a Suzanne Hart listed in the system."

"*I'm* Suzanne Hart," I shouted at her. I'd wasted enough time with this woman. A part of me knew that she was only doing her job, but another part wanted to reach across the desk and throttle her.

"Check for Dorothea Hart," Grace suggested as she put a hand on my shoulder.

"No, she's not listed either, but then again, they haven't updated the files yet from the latest arrival."

I'd taken just about all that I could stand. "Either you go back there right now and check, at least get *some* identification for the woman this instant, or I'm going to do it for you. You know what? Forget it. I'll go find out for myself."

I was about to skirt around the desk when I saw Stephen Grant coming out of the ER examination room area.

The police chief was visibly shaken, and I could see blood on his shirt from where he'd clearly cradled the injured woman against him.

"Is it Momma?" I asked, feeling my knees weaken as I asked the question, already knowing the answer.

"No, though it gave me a jolt when I saw her lying there.

"I'm afraid Betsy Wilkes is dead."

Chapter 7

"IT *wasn't* Momma?" I cried, feeling myself letting go of an involuntary sob.

"No, we're sure about that now," Stephen said firmly.

"But are you *positive*?" Grace asked him.

"One hundred percent. Betsy's face was in pretty rough shape, but it's clear enough now that it isn't your mother. I've been trying to call you," he added.

"My phone was dead," I said numbly.

"Why didn't you call *me*?" Grace asked him.

"I kind of had my hands full at the time," he said gloomily. "Suzanne, you should go find your mother and give her a hug," the police chief said.

"I can't believe an accident like that happened right in town," I said.

"Who said anything about an accident?" the chief asked me sharply.

"Are you saying that it was *deliberate*?" I asked.

"I shouldn't be saying *anything*, but it's going to get out soon enough. Myra Hickering saw the entire thing happen. She waved me down as I drove past, and as I tried to help Betsy, she told me that it was obvious that whoever did it *meant* to hit her."

"Did she get a license plate, or a description at least?" Grace asked.

"She was too busy running out into the yard, trying to help Betsy," the chief replied. "All she can swear to is that the car was a dark color, maybe some kind of SUV. It had tinted windows, so she couldn't even see who was driving."

"But she was sure that it was deliberate?" Grace asked him.

"She seemed certain enough of it at the time," the chief said. "I tried to help Betsy, but I couldn't do anything for her."

Grace put a hand on his shoulder, and I saw him flinch for an instant. "It wasn't your fault, Stephen."

"I know that, but I still don't have to like it," he said woodenly. Glancing down at his blood-splotched shirt, he said, "I've got to go back to the station to change."

"Stephen," Grace said, clearly wanting him to stay, but he just kept walking hurriedly toward the exit.

"Can't talk," he said as he waved a hand in the air. "One of my deputies is coming to pick me up," he added gruffly, and then he was gone.

"Did you just see that?" Grace asked me as she watched her boyfriend disappear. "He completely blew me off."

"Grace, he's in shock. It can't be easy to have someone die in your arms like that. Cut the man a little slack."

"Yes, you're right," she said. "So, what do we do now?"

"I'm going to take the police chief's advice and find my mother. When I do, I'm going to wrap her up in a bear hug that's so tight she might have to come back here to have a few ribs taped up when I'm finished with her."

"I'm coming with you, because I want to be next in line," she said.

"Momma, why haven't you been answering your phone?" I asked as I rushed into her cottage. She looked startled by the abrupt question, but it was nothing compared to the way she reacted to my overpowering embrace. "I thought I'd lost you."

"Suzanne, I left my phone in the car by accident. You're overreacting."

"You haven't heard the news, have you?" I asked her.

"About what in particular?"

"Someone hit Betsy Wilkes with their car while she was out on her afternoon walk. It happened four houses down the block, so how could you *not* know?"

"If you must know, I was taking a nap," Momma admitted. "The Stephenson children were playing in the yard behind me, and they were so loud that I had to turn my fan on high and my ambient music full blast to get any peace at all. I understand wanting to homeschool your children, but young Lisa has a particularly shrill squeal that can shatter glass."

"You didn't hear the ambulances *or* the fire trucks?" Grace asked her as she took her turn hugging my mother. "Exactly how loud was it in here, and just how soundly do you sleep, Dot?"

"Apparently soundly enough to miss everything. Poor Betsy. How she loved her walks. But Suzanne, why were you so worried about me?"

"Her face was unrecognizable from the accident, and from what we were told, the people first on the scene assumed it was you," I said.

"I don't walk recreationally all that much," Momma said. "Besides, I find it difficult to believe that Betsy could be mistaken for me. We look nothing alike."

"Where'd you get that jacket?" I asked her suddenly, recognizing the bold red-and-black plaid material draped loosely over one chair, exactly like the one I'd seen Betsy wearing earlier.

"It was on sale at the new boutique on the road to Union Square. It's sporty, isn't it?"

"Yes, and apparently you're not the only one who liked it. Betsy was wearing that same jacket this morning when we spoke," I said. "Momma, that hit-and-run was meant for you."

"Nonsense," Momma said after a brief hesitation. "I'm sure you're wrong."

"I'm not so sure about that myself," Grace said. "Dot, from a distance, you two could have been twins."

"Her face wasn't hidden from view when the driver hit her, was it?" Momma asked pointedly. It was clear she was uncomfortable with the notion that someone might actually be after her.

"No, but her back was turned to the road, and Myra Hickering said that she saw it happen from her window. We need to get you out of here," I told her.

"Myra isn't the most credible source in the world. And besides, even if it's true, we've already discussed that option, and I declined your invitation."

"Okay, have it your way. If you won't come back to the cottage with me, then I'm going to stay here with you," I said, inviting myself, not really caring if I was welcome or not.

"Perhaps, but we'll table that discussion until after dinner," she said firmly.

It may have worked when I'd been a child, but as Grace had reminded me earlier, I was a grown woman now. This discussion wasn't over, no matter how much she might want it to be.

Grace could read the mood in the room, so she clearly decided that it was time to cut the tension that had grown so strong since we'd come in. "Something smells delightful."

"It's a new recipe I'm trying out," she said with a smile.

"As long as it's not white chicken chili, I can't wait," I said.

Momma's expression faltered for a moment. "Suzanne, how could you possibly know that was what I made for our meal tonight?"

"A lucky guess, maybe?" I asked her.

"I don't think so."

"We had some for lunch at the diner," Grace admitted. "I'm sure yours will be delightful, too."

Momma frowned for a moment. "I ran into Hilda a few days ago at the grocery store, and she told me she was working on a recipe, but she hadn't quite perfected it yet. It intrigued me, so I started playing with a variation of my own. Never mind, we can eat something else. I'm sure I've got enough leftovers in the fridge to feed us all."

"If it's all the same to you, I'd like to try your chili," I said.

"You already told me that you didn't want it," Momma reminded me with a hint of hurt in her voice.

"I was just teasing," I assured her. I certainly wouldn't have planned it for our meal after having a variation of it at lunch, but I'd eat every bite of it, and smile as I was doing it. After all, I wasn't about to deny my mother anything so soon after being afraid that I'd lost her forever. "Honestly, it sounds great."

She looked unsure, but before she could say anything, Grace added, "I'd love some, too. I wanted seconds at lunch, but I was afraid that I'd be too full to investigate. May we *please* have some, Dot? I don't know about Suzanne, but I'm starving."

That did the trick. I knew there was no way my mother would refuse to feed us, given that particular plea. "Very well. I made some cheddar chive bread to go with it, too."

"That sounds wonderful," I said. "Let's eat."

"I don't suppose you had that type of bread at the diner, did you?" Momma asked.

"No, ma'am," I answered, not wanting to tell her that Trish had made an artisanal loaf herself. "Do you want us to catch you up on what we've been doing, or should we wait until after we eat?"

"I'd rather wait, if you two don't mind. I've already heard enough distressing news as it is. Poor Betsy."

"I feel the exact same way. You just never know, do you?"

"What do you mean by that?" Momma asked me, her voice sporting a bit of edge to it. Did she think I was referring to her age somehow?

"It's just that she was fine this morning, and now she's gone," I replied. "If that doesn't define how fleeting life can be, I don't know what does." I was careful not to make any reference to the fact that Betsy may have been murdered simply because of her resemblance to my mother, no matter how much I believed it to be true.

Momma accepted my explanation, and we all went into the kitchen together. "I thought we could eat out here instead of at the dining room table," Momma said. "I thought it would feel more homey that way."

"I eat in the kitchen every chance I get," I agreed. Momma had set the small dinette for three places. It was a bit crowded, her being used to eating there with just her husband, but none of us seemed to mind. The smells coming from the stove were amazing, and I couldn't wait to taste her efforts, since she was an amazing cook and baker in addition to her business prowess.

"Then let's eat," she said. She ladled out a small bowl and handed it to Grace. She took it, though I could see she'd been surprised by the minimal portion.

"Momma, I want more than that, and I'm willing to bet that Grace does, too," I said as she tried to do the same thing to me.

"You're both just being polite, and I know it."

I looked at her and frowned. "When have you *ever* known me to be polite when it comes to food?"

Momma considered that statement for a moment, and then she reached for Grace's bowl to add more.

"It's fine, Dot," she protested, but Momma continued to hold out her hand, and my best friend finally complied with the unspoken request.

After we each got a larger serving, I grinned. "Now we're talking."

Momma started to say something, but instead, she just laughed. "You'll be the death of me yet, young lady."

"Maybe, but I sincerely hope that it won't be for a very long time." I held the bowl up to my nose and took a deep breath. There were certainly similarities to the aroma of the Boxcar Grill's chicken chili, but there was enough different about it too that made me eager to taste it.

Momma dished out some for herself, and then she cut some slices of warm cheddar chive loaf and placed them on plates at each setting.

"If you could bottle the aromas coming out of this kitchen right now, you'd make a fortune," Grace said as she took it all in.

"I'm not at all sure who would buy such a scent," Momma said, though it was clear that she was pleased with the comment.

"Are you kidding?" I asked her. "Let a single gal dab some of that behind her ears, and she'll have to beat the men off with a ladle."

As we took our places, Momma surprised me by reaching out her hands to each of us. "May we have a moment of silence for our lost friend?"

"Certainly," Grace said, and I echoed the sentiment. Momma's idea of religion was quite a bit more private than most folks, but I knew that deep inside, her beliefs were strong. It was really special having her share them with us, two of the people she was closest to in the world, and I knew that Betsy's abrupt demise had shaken her more than she'd been letting on.

We held hands in silence, and I saw Momma and Grace both close their eyes in reflection. I was about to do the same when I noticed Momma mouthing a nearly silent prayer, and I closed my eyes as well, saying a small prayer of my own. I might not have started this investigation with Betsy in mind, but it was going to be in a very real part of it now. I vowed that I was going to do everything in my power to find out who'd run her down and make sure they were brought to justice.

"Now, let's eat," Momma said as she pulled her hands away.

"Dot, this is amazing. How did you make this?" Grace asked as she ate a second spoonful.

"I found half a dozen recipes online, and then I started tweaking them to suit my tastes. When Phillip comes home, I'll have a new meal to feed him, though that version is going to be quite a bit spicier than this one. I like a bit of a kick on occasion, but my husband enjoys the full mule."

I laughed, and Momma looked at me quizzically. "What's so funny?"

"That sounded just like something Betsy might have said," I replied with a smile.

Momma joined in. "The woman certainly had a way with language, didn't she? She once told me that she was so hungry she could eat a football with a pair of spoons, and on another occasion, we were at a church flea market when she announced to one and all that she was hotter than a candle in a forest fire, and would someone please open a door before we all passed out."

I nearly said something I shouldn't have about Betsy's murder at that point, so instead, I jammed a piece of buttered cheddar chive bread into my mouth. When all else failed, it was never a bad idea *not* to express every thought that came into my mind, or so I'd been told on more than one occasion as a child, by more people than my parents, though they'd both certainly conveyed the same sentiment themselves often enough.

"How's the bread?" Momma asked me. "I ask because from the size of the bite you just took, I'm assuming that you're still trying to take a bit of time to taste it before you wolf it all down at once."

Wow, even trying to do the right thing, I'd managed to spark a hint of disapproval. The irony of it made me smile, and after I swallowed and could speak again, I said, "What can I say? It's so good I can't stop eating it. Have you tried dipping it into the soup?"

"It's supposed to be chili," Momma reminded me.

"Isn't that what chili is?" I asked her. "But seriously, I was expecting a thick, hearty stew-like consistency, but this is almost like a rich soup instead."

Momma frowned. "I may have used too much chicken stock."

"If it were me, I wouldn't change a thing," I said. "I think it's perfect just the way it is."

"Grace, what do you think?"

My friend laid her spoon down and wiped her mouth before speaking. "Dot, I'd rather take a beating by three husky men than disagree with you, but Suzanne is right. I don't care what you call this. It's amazing! You could give Hilda lessons, I know that much."

Momma smiled. "Enough, you two. It's good, I'll grant you that much, but I'm nowhere near ready to call this recipe finished."

"Do me a favor, would you? If you need a taste tester for any more batches, give me a call, would you?" I asked her.

"Call me, too," Grace chimed in. "There isn't any more, is there?"

"Would you honestly like seconds?" she asked.

"Yes, but I'm afraid I can't. I have an appointment later."

Momma glanced at the clock. "This late? Who could you possibly be meeting at this hour?"

"Momma, it's not that late," I said calmly. "She's meeting Stephen."

"Are you talking about your boyfriend, our esteemed chief of police? Wouldn't you call that a date, my dear?"

"Ordinarily yes, but this sounded more like an appointment to me when he asked to see me," Grace admitted. "I hate to eat and run, but I need some time to get ready for whatever's coming." As she stood, she asked, "Suzanne, are you okay with bringing your mother up to speed on your own?"

"Of course. Would you like a ride home?"

"You know what? I think I'd really rather walk. I can use the time to clear my head."

We were a good two miles from her house, but I wasn't about to try to dissuade her. "Call me after, no matter what, okay?"

I hugged her, and then she hugged Momma after thanking me. "Dinner was delicious."

"I'm glad you enjoyed it," my mother told her. "Grace, no matter how dire things may seem at the moment, just remember that tomorrow is never far away, and with it fresh hope."

"Thank you," she said and then hugged Momma again. "I'm so glad you're okay."

"As am I," Momma agreed.

"How did you know that Grace was so upset?" I asked her as we cleared away the dishes.

"Daughter dear, it doesn't take a psychic to see she's troubled. What's going on with the two of them?"

"She doesn't know yet, but I have a feeling she's about to find out," I said.

Momma took that in. "She'll be all right. After all, she's got you in her corner, and that's more than anyone could hope for."

"Thanks for saying that. I really appreciate it," I said. "Do you want to wash or dry?" She had a dishwasher, but when it was just the two of us, we often washed the dishes by hand ourselves. It was an excellent time to talk about just about anything, and I treasured those moments more than I could say.

"Ordinarily I'd be delighted to take you up on your kind offer, but you've been patient enough with me. Let's load these things in the dishwasher and go into the living room. I'm not sure I can wait another moment to find out what you've uncovered so far."

Chapter 8

"THE TRUTH IS THAT I'M afraid we weren't able to come up with much," I admitted, though I did as she suggested and helped her load the dishwasher before we walked into the other room.

"Suzanne, I don't expect miracles. After all, you two can only do so much, given your complete and utter lack of authority to force anyone to speak with you."

"We did better than that," I protested. "Cordelia broke her leg, or so she says. We're going to follow up on that to be sure she's not just faking it, but it looks legitimate enough to us. Francis made a good point when we spoke with her. She said that if she were going to threaten you, it would be quite a bit different than the note you got. Still, we're not writing her off yet, either."

"And did you speak with Ellie Westmore?" Momma asked grimly.

"We did. She basically said that she thought it was all in your overactive imagination."

"I didn't *imagine* her behavior, and neither did Phillip," Momma said curtly as she sat up straighter.

"Hey, I'm on your side, remember? Don't worry. We're looking into it."

Momma settled back down into her chair. "Please forgive the outburst. Perhaps I've sent you both on a fool's errand. Chief Grant is probably right. The note I received is probably just one of many some miscreant left to get a rise out of me."

"I don't think so," I told her solemnly.

"And why not?"

"The notes themselves were different, for one thing. As far as we can tell, everyone else's was very specific, and yours was more of a general threat. Next, the paper and the font used were both different, and finally, the places the notes were left were different. Everyone else got a note in their mailbox; yours was the only one taped to the doorbell. Momma, someone's not very happy with you, and I think they may have escalated things to murder when they mistook Betsy Wilkes for you out on that sidewalk in front of Myra's house."

"I still believe that's utter nonsense. I refuse to believe that it was anything but an accident," Momma said. "Threatening me is one thing, but murder? I haven't ever made anyone *that* angry."

"At least as far as you know," I told her. "How do you explain the hit-and-run, then? You two had the same hairstyle, the identical build, and you were both even wearing the same jacket, for goodness' sake. How can you *not* see that it was an attempt on your life, not Betsy's?"

I hadn't meant to be so brutal, but what choice did I have? Momma needed to take this seriously, deadly seriously, and if I had to rub her nose in it, then so be it.

"Let me ponder that awhile, Suzanne. Were you able to discover anything else? Not that I'm expecting you to. You've done quite a bit in such a limited amount of time."

"Well, we went to Maple Hollow to speak with Gerard Mince, but he was out of the office, or so his receptionist said. We're fairly certain that he slipped out the back when he saw us there and drove away before we could talk to him." As I told her that, I thought about Myra's description of the car that had struck Betsy. The car we'd seen at Mince's business had indeed been a dark SUV, but that didn't necessarily mean anything. After all, there were a great many of those vehicles on the road. Then again, Myra could have gotten a few of the details wrong. After all, she'd just seen a woman mowed down right in front of her, so a few lapses in accuracy could be forgiven.

"Well, well. You *have* been busy," she answered.

"Oh, and Max is missing, too," I said.

I was about to tell her about the elopement when she interrupted me. "*Your* Max?"

"Momma, he hasn't been *my* Max for a long time," I corrected her. "And besides, he's *Emily's* Max now. They eloped a few days ago."

Momma looked unhappy. "Suzanne. I'm so sorry."

"Why? I've got Jake, and as far as I'm concerned, I traded up big-time. I want them to be happy. Everyone deserves a shot at that."

"You're not the least bit bitter about it?" Momma asked me.

"Not even a little." It made me feel good knowing that I was telling her the truth.

"What's this about him missing, then?" she asked me.

"Emily told me that he was going to tell me about their sudden marriage, and she thinks he might just be lying low until she finally has no choice but to tell me herself."

"That sounds exactly like something Max would do," Momma said dismissively. "No doubt he'll turn up later when he learns that the deed has been done."

"No doubt," I said. I took a deep breath, and then I added, "I know you really don't want to think about what happened to Betsy, but we need to at least discuss it."

"Yes, I can see that," Momma said after frowning for a few moments. "So let's talk about what happened to her. I'm willing to sit here quietly and listen to your theories now."

I wasn't about to pass up that opportunity. "First off, let's look at the possibilities. It *could* have been an accident."

"That's what I think," Momma said, breaking her vow of silence immediately.

Ignoring her, I continued, "With the way people text and drive these days, it's got to be a possibility, but what are the odds that whoever was driving chose that precise moment to look away from the road? Could they have dropped their phone, or spilled a drink? Maybe, but why accelerate, as Myra indicated they did? It sounds like an awfully big coincidence to me."

"And yet coincidences happen every day," Momma reminded me.

"Sure, but for the purposes of our investigation, thinking that doesn't do us any good, so let's move on to some less pleasant reasons for the hit-and-run."

"*All* of them are unpleasant," Momma said as she shook her head.

"Granted, but remember, we're exploring possibilities. One other idea is that whoever did it knew perfectly well who they were going after. Did Betsy Wilkes have any enemies?"

"Betsy? I can't imagine," Momma said, clearly puzzled by the very idea. "Who on earth would have any reason to want to harm *Betsy*?"

"Maybe nobody, but you'd be surprised. Grace and I will do some digging into her life just to rule out that possibility." I took a deep breath before I added, "The last scenario we need to consider is that whoever killed Betsy was coming after you."

Momma didn't protest. Instead, she slumped back into her chair even further. For a woman who prided herself on her posture, who constantly commanded me as a child to sit up straight, it was rather telling. "I admit there's an air of uncertainty there. As you so aptly pointed out, there were several similarities in our appearances, and that cursed jacket was probably the final touch." She stood and walked over to it. "I'm afraid I'll never be able to wear it again. I can't stand the very sight of it anymore. Suzanne, will you take care of it for me?"

I nodded. "Just leave it there, and I'll grab it on my way out."

"Thank you. So, what do we do now? It's too late to investigate any further, and besides, you have to be up early to run the donut shop in the morning."

"At least I don't have to worry about that. It's Emma and Sharon's turn tomorrow and the next day." I had originally allowed my assistant and her mother to run Donut Hearts a few days a week so I could spend more time with Jake, but that had been mainly because he was retired. Now that he was consulting, I might have to rethink the arrangement. After all, I needed something to do with my time, and we could use the money; there was no doubt about that. Still, I knew that Emma was paying for college while Sharon was accumulating funds for one of her many trips abroad, so it wouldn't be fair to penalize the two of them. We'd work something out, but for the moment, I was glad for the break so I could devote my energy to the investigation.

"Suzanne?" Momma asked, bringing me back to reality.

"Sorry about that. Like I said, I've got the shop covered for the next few days."

"What about Grace? Will she be free to help you? Or will she even be in the right frame of mind to pitch in?"

"We don't have to worry about her. She won't let me down," I said, knowing that it was true. No matter what was going on in her life, Grace would be there for me. It was something I counted on with as much assurance as knowing that the sun would come up tomorrow in the east.

"Still," Momma said, the simple word carrying powerful meaning.

"Still," I said with assurance. "Now let's talk about you."

"What about me?" Momma asked. "I've already told you that I'm not going to come to the cottage and stay with you, Suzanne. That's final."

"Then I'll have to stay here," I said. "Now that Phillip has taken over your guestroom for his research materials, I suppose the couch will have to do."

"Suzanne, you really don't need to stay here with me," she said, scolding me. "I'm a grown woman."

"Momma, let's consider the possibility that our worst fear about what really happened to Betsy is on the money. What do you think the killer is going to do once they realize they ran the wrong woman down? Do you think this gives you a free pass or something? Now they are more focused than ever to get rid of you. They've already committed one murder. There's no going back now."

"You make it all sound so ominous," Momma said.

"Good. It's intentional. Now, unless I'm mistaken, I've still got a toothbrush and a change of clothes in the Jeep. Let me trot out and get them, and I'll be all set."

Momma frowned a moment before finally relenting. "Do you have clean sheets in the upstairs bedroom at the cottage?"

"You know I do," I said. "I was well trained in the art of being a good hostess from one of the very best," I added with a grin.

"Very well. Let me pack a few things, and I'll be ready to go."

"You'll really come home with me? Thank you, Momma. You can have your old bedroom back, and I'll take mine upstairs."

"Nonsense. I am to be *your* visitor. The upstairs bedroom will be perfect for my needs."

I wasn't about to quibble over such a small point, not when I'd won the main battle. "I'm okay with that, too. This means a great deal to me. I know you don't think it's necessary, but I can't tell you how happy I am that you're doing it."

Momma stopped in front of me, reached up, and patted my cheek with a great deal of affection. "That's why I'm coming with you, my sweet little girl."

I fully realized that she knew I was grown up, but it was still nice to know that she sometimes still thought of me as her sweet little girl.

I got Momma set up upstairs in my old room, and I was just getting into my pajamas when my cell phone rang. It wasn't Jake, but it was the next best thing.

"Grace, are you okay? What did Stephen say?"

"It's nothing I want to go over on the phone, but I promised you a phone call. Suzanne, I need some time to digest what just happened, but we'll talk about it tomorrow, if it's all the same to you."

I wasn't sure I'd be able to get to sleep not knowing what had happened between them, but I knew better than to push her. "Fine, but if you need me in the middle of the night, I'm just up the road. Oh, by the way, Momma came home with me after all."

"How did you manage to talk her into that? No, don't tell me. It can wait until morning. I'm calling in sick tomorrow so I can help you sort out what happened today."

"I appreciate that," I said. I knew I had to drop it, but I just couldn't help myself. "Grace, at least tell me one thing. Are you okay?"

"I'm not really sure, but thanks for asking. Until tomorrow, Suzanne."

"Bright and early," I said, and we ended the call.

I had a hunch that it hadn't gone well for my best friend. She sounded as though she was still in shock, and I couldn't believe what an idiot Stephen Grant was for dumping her, but I wasn't going to say that. I'd be there for her to help her pick up the pieces of her life and start over. It had happened to both of us before, and though things had been tough at times, we'd gotten through them. That was part of what being a best friend meant, through thick and thin.

I just hated that she had to go through the pain of losing love yet again, especially when I'd been lucky enough to have Jake come into my life at exactly the right time.

I had just fallen asleep again when my cell phone rang once more. Sitting up in bed, I gave my head a quick shake, and then I tried to put on my best happy voice. "Jake! I'm so glad you called."

"I woke you up, didn't I?" my husband asked.

"What? Nonsense. I won't be asleep for hours yet."

"Suzanne, don't lie to me," he answered, and I could hear the smile in his voice as he said it. "I knew I was pushing things calling this late, but I just got a few minutes free for the first time today. How are things going in April Springs?"

"Absolutely fine," I lied. "How's your case going?"

"It's a puzzler, but I'm making progress. Things aren't fine there at all, are they?"

How could he read my tone of voice so well? "I miss you."

"I miss you, too, but something happened." There was no question in his voice, just a flat statement. "Talk, woman."

I sighed. "Somebody left Momma a threatening note taped to her doorbell, and Grace and I are trying to figure out who did it."

"What did it say?" Jake asked sternly. "Do you need me to come back home?"

"No, we're handling it," I said. "You can't just walk out on your first real consulting case. We're already making some progress."

"Read the note to me," he said without commenting about whether he would or would not be coming back to April Springs. That was one of the reasons I hadn't wanted to tell him. My husband was nearly as protective of my mother as he was of me, and that was saying something.

"'*I know what you did, and you aren't going to get away with it.*'" As I repeated the words, they still gave me a chill, and I had to wonder if they weren't a precursor to murder.

"What did she have to say about it?" Jake asked.

"She doesn't believe it's all that serious. Someone has been leaving notes all over town making all kinds of wild statements and accusations. Chief Grant isn't taking it too seriously."

"Okay, I get that. Is there anything else going on?"

I knew better than to lie to him when he asked a question like that. "Someone hit Betsy Wilkes with their car and then fled the scene." What I neglected to mention was how closely Betsy resembled Momma, at least superficially.

"That's the lowest form of cowardice, as far as I'm concerned," Jake said.

I yawned despite trying to stifle it, and of course he picked up on it immediately.

"I'm sorry to call you so late. I just wanted to hear a friendly voice. I love you, Suzanne."

"I love you, too. Are you okay?"

"Fine and dandy," he lied. He wasn't the only one who could read the tone of his spouse's voice.

"Liar," I said with a laugh.

"It's just taking a little time getting used to being back on the job," he replied. "I'll adjust."

"If you don't, there's no shame in coming home," I told him.

For some reason, that made him chuckle. "Yeah, right. Sleep tight, my love."

"You, too," I said.

I probably should have told him more about our suspicions that Betsy's murder had been tied into our investigation about the threat against my mother, but it hadn't been the right time. Besides, I knew we'd talk again soon, and maybe, hopefully, next time I'd have something more concrete to add to my suspicions.

For now, all I could do was get some sleep so I'd be able to tackle the case the next day with fresh eyes.

Chapter 9

TO MY SURPRISE, I AWOKE the second time that morning to hear voices coming from somewhere in my cottage. I'd woken up the first time at my normal hour, what was the middle of the night for most folks, but I'd trained myself to fall back asleep, and that was what I'd done.

How long had I slept, anyway? I glanced at my clock and saw that it was just a bit past seven. Wow, I must have been in some kind of sleep coma to stay in bed that long. I couldn't remember doing that since I'd been a teen. I grabbed my robe and slippers and headed out to see what all the fuss was about.

"Wow, that smells amazing," I said as I walked into the kitchen to find Momma cooking breakfast and Grace sitting at the kitchen table. "I love your pancakes, Momma."

"You slept so long that I was about to call the paramedics," my mother said.

"Did I seriously beat you up?" Grace asked with a slight smile. "I'm going to have to race home and put that in my diary so I don't forget."

"How are you doing? Did you sleep well?" I asked her as I sat at the place that had been set for me.

"I'm good," she said, though she grimaced for a split second before she said it. I got the message. She would talk to me about what had happened, but not in front of Momma. "How about you?"

"Me? Apparently I got over nine hours of sleep," I admitted, "and I only woke up once. Is this what it feels like to be well rested?"

"You should do it more often," my mother said. No matter how close we'd become as adults, there were times when that motherly voice still forced its way out.

"Agreed," I said. "When will those pancakes be ready?"

"In thirty seconds," she said. Even given the circumstances, I could tell that my mother was happy to be there, and to be serving us a meal. There was something about the act of feeding me that never failed to please her.

As she placed pancakes in front of each of us, I asked, "Aren't you eating?"

"I'll wait until you two are finished," she said.

"I don't think so," I said as I pulled one of the two pancakes off my plate and slid it onto hers. Grace grinned as she followed suit.

"Girls, I appreciate the thought, but who will make the next batch?"

"We'll take turns," I said as I put a little butter on my pancake, added some syrup, and then picked it up with my hands and folded it in half, as though it were a taco. After taking a huge bite, I put it back down on my plate and took up my mother's station at the stove.

"Suzanne Hart, I raised you better than that," Momma said with a scolding tone.

"What can I say? We all know that you did your best, but sometimes my inner self just seems to fight its way out."

"Inner child, you mean," Grace corrected me. "If you ask me, I'd say that she's around eight years old."

"Yeah, that's probably fair," I said with a smile. "I can live with that. Now sit, Momma."

My mother was about to protest, but when she saw that we were both thoroughly enjoying ourselves, she shrugged and took her seat. "I can see that I'm not going to win this argument, so I concede."

"Wow. Really?" I asked her with obvious glee.

"Don't get too cocky, Suzanne," Grace warned me as I poured three more discs of batter onto the griddle, a fresh one for each of us. "You wouldn't have won if she'd cared about the issue, and we all know it." She turned to Momma and asked, "Isn't that right, Dot?"

"My, these are good, even if I say so myself," Momma said after taking her first bite, neither confirming nor denying Grace's point.

"See? I told you so," Grace said, and then she started in on her own pancake.

We took turns after that, and by the time the batter was finished, we were all nicely full.

As I stood, Momma suggested, "Suzanne, why don't you go get dressed, and I'll clean up here?"

"I'll help you, Dot," Grace said.

"I'm not going to go and leave this mess to both of you," I insisted.

"It's fine," Grace said. "The sooner you get ready, the faster we can get started on our day."

I could see that they were both adamant about their plan, so I knew that the best thing I could do was to just comply with their wishes. "Fine, I give up. Momma, what are you going to do today?"

She looked shocked by my question. "Why, I'm going to work. What else would I do?"

"I was kind of hoping you'd hang out here all day with the doors locked and the shades pulled," I admitted.

"Nonsense. I was willing to agree to your wishes last night, but I won't hide in some hole while you two are out there risking your lives to find the truth. Besides, I have too many things I need to address that have to be done in person. Don't worry about me. I'll be perfectly safe."

"I understand you wanting to go on with your life as though nothing has happened, but at least promise me you won't see anyone today who might want you dead."

Momma smiled softly at me. "Suzanne, how could I even know exactly who that might be? The list I gave you two yesterday might not be anywhere near complete."

"Okay. Just be careful, and try not to be alone with anyone today who might wish you ill. Can you at least do that for me?"

"For us, Dot?" Grace added.

"You two are a pair of worrying old hens," Momma said, though it was clear that she said it with love in her heart.

"Cockadoodle doo, then," I said.

"That's a rooster crowing, not a hen," Momma corrected me.

"Doesn't matter," I replied. "Just watch your back. We don't want to lose you."

"I'll promise that much, at least," Momma said.

"Then I'll go take a shower and get ready to start sleuthing again," I conceded. "Oh, I need to stop by Donut Hearts first thing. I need to remind Emma that we need to reorder from our supplier today. We're running low on flour and yeast."

"Can't she just pop in at the grocery store if she runs out?" Grace asked.

"Not and get the prices we get from our supplier," I said. "Our margin is razor thin as it is. We can't afford to pay full retail prices on *anything* and still stay afloat. When we buy in bulk, we get a huge discount, and it makes all of the difference in the world to our profit margins."

"A stop at the donut shop it is, then," Grace said. "Just go get ready."

"Yes, ma'am," I agreed.

"Momma, are you sure you won't stay here and keep a low profile today?" I asked as I rejoined them in the living room. The kitchen had been made tidy again, cleaner than I probably kept it, truth be told, and they were enjoying an early-morning fire in the hearth. I knew there was a great deal of convenience in having gas logs in a fireplace, and they were certainly a lot neater than burning real wood, but there was something about an actual fire that I loved.

"I will do my best not to antagonize anyone any more than I have to," she said. "Don't you have things to do?"

"Suzanne, it's the best we're going to be able to get out of her," Grace said with a shrug. "I think we should take it and run."

"You're right. Are you ready?"

"I'm right behind you," Grace said as she stood and joined me at the door.

"Be careful, ladies," Momma reminded us.

"Right back at you."

"I always am," she said with a slight smile, and then we left the cottage together, eager to continue our investigation.

The second we were outside though, I stopped and turned to Grace. "Are you ready to tell me what happened last night?"

"Nothing much," she said nonchalantly. "How about you?"

"Grace, don't even try to be funny. Did Stephen break up with you?"

She got into the Jeep, and I had no choice but to follow suit, especially if I wanted to continue the conversation.

"No," she said simply.

"Then what happened?"

"He proposed."

Chapter 10

"CONGRATULATIONS," I said as the relief flooded through me. I'd been so sure that he was about to end things between them that I hadn't even allowed myself to consider other, more pleasant outcomes. It wasn't that I thought Grace *had* to be married, to Stephen Grant or anyone else for that matter, but I knew that she was happier with him in her life, so why shouldn't she embrace it?

"Not so fast," Grace said grimly.

Then I got the hesitation. "Did you turn him down? Seriously? I thought that was what you wanted."

"So did I, until he actually got down on one knee and asked."

"Wow, I'm not afraid to admit that I did not see that coming."

"Neither did Stephen," she said.

Trying to put the best light on things, I said, "Don't worry, Grace. I'm sure there's *someone* out there for you."

She looked confused by my statement. "I'm sorry, I wasn't clear. Suzanne, I didn't say no."

"Then I'm puzzled," I said. "What exactly *did* you say?"

"I told him that I needed some time to think about it," she explained. "That's got to be better than an outright no, wouldn't you say?"

"I suppose it depends on your final answer, but I understand what you're saying. How did he react?"

Grace frowned for a moment before she spoke. "Obviously he wasn't thrilled, but he understood. At least he said that he did. Things are complicated, and that's what I told him. It's taken me a long time to reach this stage in my life, and I want to be absolutely certain that I make the right decision."

"I understand, but Grace, if you wait until you're *absolutely* certain, it might be too late."

She nodded. "I understand that, and if it is, I'm willing to live with the consequences. Now can we *please* not talk about this anymore? I don't want to think about *anything* but the case we're working on, at least not for the next few hours. Is that okay with you?"

"Absolutely," I said. "Are you sure you don't mind if we go by Donut Hearts first?"

"No, I already said that was okay with me," she said. "No more food for me, though. I'm stuffed. I can't believe how many pancakes we ate this morning."

"They're kind of addicting, aren't they? I don't think Emma and Sharon will be offended if we don't sample their donuts this morning."

"Good, because I think if I tried to take another bite, I'd explode."

"We could always push lunch later if you think you might be too full to eat," I said.

"Hang on, let's not do anything rash. I'm sure by lunchtime, I'll be ready to eat again, no matter how much I protest to the contrary at the moment."

I had to laugh. "Where do you put it? I swear you eat more than I do on a daily basis, and yet you've somehow managed to keep your trim figure, while I seem to gain inches and pounds with every bite."

"I attribute it to clean living and a strong sense of self," she said with a smile. "That and my DNA. I don't know what you're complaining about. Sometimes I feel as though I'm all angles, but you are *full* of pleasing curves. I think you have an adorable figure, Suzanne."

"Thanks, but I'd kill to have yours," I answered.

"Isn't that the way of it? We each want what the other one has. Now, after the donut shop, what are our plans?"

"I'd like to go back to Maple Hollow and corner Gerard Mince first."

"What if he's not in his office, or worse yet, he tries to run away again?" she asked me as I parked in front of where Gabby Williams's old shop, ReNEWed, used to be. The bulldozers had come in and removed the remnants of the building, bringing the lot back to bare earth again, and someone had even planted grass. It was almost as though Gabby's gently used clothing shop had never existed. I'd had hopes that she'd rebuild on her old spot, but the last I'd heard, she was in Hawaii, enjoying the sizeable insurance settlement she'd gotten from the fire that had destroyed her business. Maybe she'd come back to us, and perhaps she'd even start over with a new business, but with Gabby, I knew that the *only* thing that was certain was that she would do whatever *she* pleased, and the world around her, and their expectations, could go bark at the moon, as far as she was concerned.

There was a nice crowd inside Donut Hearts when we walked in the door, and I tried to stifle my jealousy. Were that many folks eating there when *I* was running things on a daily basis? Probably, but I still felt a twinge knowing that someone else had been able to step into my shoes without missing a beat, at least as far as my customers were concerned. Was I even needed at my own shop anymore?

That question was dispelled the moment I saw Emma's face.

"Thank goodness you're here, Suzanne. I need you," she said frantically.

It took everything I had not to smile. "What's going on?"

"We're running low on flour and yeast, and I can't find the supplier's contact information anywhere. Before you ask, I checked your desk, but I couldn't find anything. Then I got a call that a woman from Hickory had heard about us from a friend, and she's bringing her garden club here at ten o'clock this morning! She expects us to hold eight dozen donuts just for her, but by then, I doubt I'll be able to scrape up two or three. Then there's Ellie Westmore."

"What about Ellie?" I asked.

"She came in here asking to see you, and when I told her that it was your day off, she got upset. Obviously she's troubled about something. What did you do to her, Suzanne? I had her in the third grade, and I never so much as heard her raise her voice."

"How did you leave things with her?" I asked Emma, not wanting to get into our investigation of who had threatened Momma *or* where I'd left things with my former teacher.

"She said she'd be back at eleven, and that she was expecting you to be here," Emma said. "I swear, seeing her gave me the chills. I felt like a little kid again."

I smiled at the news. "She tends to have that effect on people she once taught, but give it time. You'll get over it."

"Are you sure?" Emma asked me. It was clear that she was still intimidated by our old teacher.

"I'm positive." I looked around and couldn't spot her mother anywhere. "Is Sharon in back?" I asked.

"That's another problem. She had a doctor's appointment she couldn't miss that she forgot to tell me about until fifteen minutes ago," Emma said. "She should be back in half an hour."

"Emma, why didn't you call me?" I asked her as I grabbed my old apron. Before she could answer, I turned to Grace. "Sorry, but I need forty-five minutes."

"That's perfect. I can go home and dive into my paperwork. The truth is that you're doing me a favor. I can change my sick day to a work day, so it's a win-win situation as far as I'm concerned."

"Will your boss actually let you do that?" I asked her.

"My numbers are so good right now that I can pretty much do whatever I please," she said. "Come by the house when you're finished."

"Thanks." After she was gone, I turned to Emma. "Here's what we're going to do. You handle the front. After I order more supplies, I'll get started on the extra donuts. I'm afraid they're going to all be cake ones, since I don't have time to make a batch of yeast donuts from scratch."

"She didn't care what we served, just as long as we had *something* for her group," Emma said with a sigh of relief. "Thanks, Suzanne. You're a real lifesaver. I didn't know what to do."

"Emma, I'm hardly ever more than a phone call away."

"I know, but I wanted to do it on my own. After all, you've run the shop by yourself one day a week since your first day here."

"Yes, but it could get crazy at times without having anyone to back me up," I told her.

"I'm still waiting for my donuts," Dan Bradley, a cop on the April Springs police force, said a bit impatiently at the counter.

"Coming right up," Emma said, smiling at me briefly before turning to our customer and filling his order.

I started whipping up a decent-sized batch of cake donut batter, and while it was mixing, I got my supplier on the phone and managed to place our order in time to be delivered the next morning. I was feeling pretty good about things when Emma came back with a frown on her face.

"What's going on now?" I asked her as I divided the batter into one large bowl and one smaller one. I was going to make two dozen of our plain old-fashioned donuts, two dozen iced, two dozen cinnamon topped, and two dozen of a new apple spice recipe I'd just perfected. Fortunately, the bulk of the donuts would use the same basic recipe, but I felt as though I had to offer them at least *one* specialty donut. After all, if there were truly that many new people visiting Donut Hearts, I wanted to give at least some of them a reason to come back. "I need to get these ready."

"I'm sorry, but Chief Grant is out front, and he says that it's urgent that he talk to you."

That could be about Grace or one of the cases we were working on at the moment, but I couldn't stop what I was doing at that moment either way. "Send him back," I said as I started mixing the apple spice recipe.

"But you hate having people in the kitchen while you're working," Emma said, as though she had to remind me.

"I know, but I don't really have much choice, do I?" I tried to take the sting out of my words with a smile, but Emma still looked troubled by my small outburst. I took a deep breath, and then I said, in a much calmer voice, "Emma, you know as well as I do that things can get a little crazy here from time to time. It seems as though nothing happens at all out of the ordinary for days or even weeks on end, and then everything seems to get crazy at exactly the same moment. This just happens to be that moment this time, but don't worry, we'll get through it."

"How can you always make everything seem as though it's all going to work out?" she asked me.

"I'm glad you think so, because at times it surely doesn't feel that way to me. Now don't keep our chief of police waiting."

"I won't," she said, and then she disappeared back out front.

I didn't have time to wonder what this particular conversation was going to be about, anyway. I had to get back to work.

After all, there were donuts to be made, and they weren't going to mix themselves and hop into the fryer one by one all of their own accord.

"I didn't think you were working today," Chief Grant said as he walked into my kitchen.

I was about to answer when I looked at him closely. "When was the last time you got some sleep, Chief?"

"Two days ago. What's going on with Grace, Suzanne?"

"She's home doing paperwork for an hour while I pitch in here," I answered, sure that he was asking me an entirely different question, but if he wanted to know something more specific than that, he was going to have to come right out and ask me himself.

"I'm talking about my proposal, and you know it. Don't try to pretend like she didn't discuss it with you. You two talk about *everything*."

I shrugged. "Stephen, she gave me the highlights, but she told me she didn't want to discuss it, and I respected her wishes. Be patient with her. She just needs time to think things through."

"What's there to think about?" he asked, a hint of anguish coming out in his voice. "We love each other. Does anything else matter?"

I didn't know how to answer that question, so I ignored it. "Is she really asking for too much? She didn't say no. That's something, isn't it?"

"I'm not looking for a consolation prize. I want her to be my wife," he said gruffly. "When Jake asked you, how long did it take you to say yes?"

I wasn't about to tell him that I accepted before he even had the chance to finish his proposal. Not only would it not help the situation, but it wasn't fair. After all, every relationship was different.

"Doesn't matter. I said yes to Max immediately, and we both know how much I lived to regret that rash answer."

"You're not comparing me to Max, are you?" the police chief asked unhappily. "I would never take off without telling Grace where I was going, especially not if we were married."

"You just need to resist the impulse to push her into making a decision before she's ready," I said firmly. "That much I know. If you want a quick answer, I can almost guarantee you that it's not going to be the one you're hoping for."

"Yeah, I can see that. It's good advice, if I can find a way to take it. Thanks for that."

"You're welcome," I said as I loaded the new dropper with the plain batter and started dropping donuts into the hot oil. At least Emma had kept the vat of oil on, so I didn't have to wait for it to heat up again. "While you're here, do you mind if I ask you a few questions?"

"I can hardly refuse you right now, can I?" he asked me with a grin. I was glad to see the old Stephen shine through the gloom, if only for the briefest of moments.

"It's about the cases I'm working on," I warned him.

"Did you say cases, as in plural?" he asked me.

"They might be related, but then again, they might not," I admitted.

"Go on, ask me anything, but I reserve the right not to answer."

"Fair enough," I said. "Do you have any leads on the hit-and-run?"

"Just what we got from Myra Hickering," he acknowledged. "One other witness saw even less than she did. He heard the car jump the curb as it hit her, but by the time he turned around, he couldn't provide any more detail than Myra did."

"Who was the witness?" I asked him.

"Nope, I'm not going to tell you that," he said. "Next question."

I'd been expecting him to refuse to tell me, but I thought it had been worth a shot. "Have you discovered who's been leaving the notes around town?"

"No, but we have a few solid leads we're following up on," he answered almost by rote.

"I'm not Ray Blake writing a story for the newspaper," I reminded him. "You can tell me the truth without worrying about seeing it in the paper the next day."

"Fair enough. Okay, we've narrowed it down to three kids who might be responsible. Right now we're checking them out."

"What are their names?" I asked.

"Again, that's part of an active police investigation, so no, I'm not going to share them with you."

"I thought you weren't giving the notes much credence?" I asked him. "When did it become an active police investigation?"

"No comment," he repeated. "Next."

"My ex-husband seems to have disappeared. Do you have any information about that?"

He looked surprised to hear the news. "No one's said anything to me about it, and there haven't been any police reports filed, either. How long has he been missing?"

"Since yesterday morning," I admitted.

"Any theories about what happened to him?"

I didn't particularly want to tell him, but I didn't really have much choice. "He and Emily Hargraves eloped, and he was supposed to tell me about it before word got out around town, but Emily ended up telling me herself."

"That sounds about right," he said. "Max didn't want to face you, so he let his new wife do it. Now that you know, he'll probably turn up soon enough."

"I hope you're right, but I still wondered if you were looking into it."

"I'll ask around," Chief Grant said. "You still care about him, don't you?"

"I care about Emily, and sure, I guess to a lesser extent, I care about Max, too. After all, I'm happy. Why shouldn't he deserve the same chance?"

"What does Jake think about it?" Stephen asked me.

"He's out of town on a case. Didn't he tell you?"

"We haven't spoken in a few weeks," the chief of police said. "We usually try to have breakfast once a week just to keep in touch, but I had to cancel last week. There was a wreck out on the interstate, and I had to drive over and help out. Where did he go?"

After I named the city in Virginia, he shook his head. "Never heard of it. Good for him. He's too good to be mothballed so early."

"I couldn't agree more," I said. I'd used up my main questions, so it was time to tell him something that I didn't think he was going to be happy about hearing. "I believe that there's a good chance that whoever ran Betsy Wilkes down was really trying to kill my mother."

I half expected him to explode, but instead, he frowned for a few moments before he said, "Okay, convince me."

"They had similar builds, close haircuts, and identical jackets," I said. "Plus, according to Myra, Betsy's back was turned to the road, so whoever spotted her on her walk might have thought they were seeing

Momma instead. After all, she was struck down only four houses down from my mother's cottage."

He mulled that over for nearly a minute before he replied. "I suppose it's possible, but for the moment, we've decided to treat it like an accident."

That surprised me, and I must have shown it in my expression. "Betsy Wilkes was mowed down in cold blood, Chief, whether she was the intended victim or not. You heard what Myra said."

"Myra said a great many things," the chief said. "I started doing a little digging. Did you know that she's reported six crimes in the past three weeks, all of them false alarms? Her stories keep getting more and more outlandish, so I'm not sure how much credence we can give to her account of what really happened to Betsy. The other witness saw the car involved speeding away, but folks leave accident scenes all too often."

"What kind of crimes has she reported?" She'd seemed so lucid when we'd spoken that it surprised me to learn that she might be a bit off.

"It's all a matter of public record, since we had to file reports every time, so I don't suppose it would hurt to tell you. She claimed that there were three attempted break-ins in her storage shed in back, two suspicious-looking characters lurking in her front yard after dark, and a wolf was supposedly on her front porch the night before last. Turns out that the 'wolf' in question was Sally Granger's husky, BooBoo. The breaker tripped on his electric containment fence, and he took a tour of April Springs before Sally corralled him back into her yard. One of the suspicious characters turned out to be Sally, too. She was walking BooBoo, and he did his business on her front lawn. Sally, being a good dog owner, picked up the poo, so there you go."

"What about the shed break-ins?" I asked.

"It turned out that it was a raccoon getting into some old sunflower seeds Myra uses in the winter to feed the birds. You should see her backyard. She has more feeders back there than you can imagine during the cold months, and she was a little slipshod putting the lids back on a few of the buckets, unless the raccoon got them off himself, which is always a possibility. The point is that Myra is highly suggestible, so I'm not sure how much credence we should really give her story."

"A woman is still dead though, right? *That* wasn't something she got wrong."

"No, of course not. We're looking at all of the dark SUVs we can find, both on the tax books and on our regular patrols, but so far, we haven't seen anything suspicious."

At that moment his radio went off.

"Chief, we need you over at Myra's place again," the dispatcher said.

"What is it this time?"

"She claims that someone was trying to break into the front door this time. There's a twist, though. Her son sent her a trail camera for her birthday to take photos of her birdfeeders, and she was testing it out on the porch, so we might see exactly who it was."

"I'm on my way," he said. "Suzanne, sorry, but I've got to go."

I was finished with the donuts I'd been frying, glazing them as we chatted, so I was ready, too. "Mind if I tag along and see what was on the camera?"

"It's nothing," the chief said. "I'm sure of it."

"Then you won't mind me driving over there behind you."

The police chief didn't look particularly happy about it, but he finally just shrugged. "I don't suppose I can stop you. We're finished here, right?"

"We are as far as I'm concerned. Thanks for your help," I said.

"Thank you," he replied.

I got up on the porch as the chief pulled the memory card from the camera and put it into his laptop computer. "I've got one of these cameras at my place, too," he said.

He tapped a few keys, and then he ejected the card and put it back in place. "What did you see?" I asked him.

"It was blank," he said, and then he checked the batteries. Myra was hovering nearby, and he turned to her and explained, "The batteries were in backwards. Let me flip them around for you." After he took them out and put them back in the correct way, he asked her, "See that little light? That means it's working."

"So whoever was on my porch got away with trespassing," she said with a frown.

"It's not exactly the crime of the century, Myra," the chief said, doing his best to hide the exasperation in his voice.

"What are you saying, that invading my property isn't a crime anymore?" she asked him sharply.

"Your land's not even posted, Myra," he replied. "Anyway, call us if you need us. You know the number, right?"

"Don't get smart with me, young man."

"Sorry," he apologized, though it was clear his heart wasn't in it. "You have a good day now, you hear?"

"You, too," she said, mollified at least a bit by his apology.

"See what I mean?" Chief Grant asked as we parted ways. "Stay safe, Suzanne."

"You do the same, Chief," I told him, then I got back into my Jeep and headed straight to Grace's place. I'd done what I'd needed to do at Donut Hearts, and Emma had settled down quite a bit after her mother had returned to the shop. I couldn't blame my assistant for being in a bit of a tizzy. It was a lot to deal with handling the front *and* the back of the shop at the same time, and that unexpected order would have thrown me off my game a bit, too. Now that Donut Hearts was covered though, I could go on investigating with Grace with a clear conscience.

My business was in good hands, and I was going to do my best to see that our investigations, both of them, moved forward.

Chapter 11

"I WASN'T EXPECTING you so soon," Grace said when I came to her door and rang the bell.

"There was a change in plans," I said. "Stephen came by the shop."

Grace's expression clouded up. "I told him I needed some time, so what does he do? He runs crying to you about me."

"Take it easy," I told her. "He was there about the cases we're working on." That might not have been entirely true, but we had discussed a great many possibilities, and I felt as though I owed him that much, covering his back with Grace.

She didn't seem to be buying it, though. "And you didn't talk about me at all?"

I wasn't going to lie so blatantly to her, not even for our police chief. "I never said that."

"What did you tell him?"

"That he should listen to you and do as you ask, give you some space so you can make the decision that's right for you."

"Okay, I'm sorry I jumped the gun. Was he much help in our two cases?"

"He did his best, but I don't think he knows much, either, and what he does know, he's not at liberty to discuss with us," I admitted. "It turns out that Myra isn't all that reliable as a witness, based on her past and present performances. She set up a trail camera on her front porch to catch whoever's been stalking her—her words not mine—but she had the batteries in backwards. Evidently she's been reporting a veritable crime spree around her place, from loose dog-wolves to rampant raccoons. The chief isn't sure he can take *anything* she tells him without a grain of salt."

"How about the car?"

"They're looking for it," I said.

"And the source of the threatening notes?" she asked as she walked down to my Jeep with me.

"He has three younger suspects, but he wouldn't share any names with me."

"Well, he can't really do that, can he?" she asked.

"Oh, and nobody told him that Max was missing, so he's going to keep an eye out for him, too," I said as I started the vehicle. "We're going straight to Maple Hollow, right?"

"That sounds good to me," she said. "Suzanne, are you worried at all about Max?"

"I can't help but be a *little* concerned," I admitted, "but that's on the back burner for now. We need to see who threatened Momma, and find the car that killed Betsy Wilkes."

"In that order?" she asked me.

"I've got a feeling that it's one and the same person, so it's not really like we have two tasks," I admitted. "Everyone else can think whatever they want to, but I know in my heart that hit-and-run was meant for Momma, and I'm going to prove it."

"What if it wasn't, though?" Grace asked softly as I passed the newspaper building and then the bank on my way to Maple Hollow.

"Even if they were unrelated, I still want to find whoever did both things," I admitted, "but finding Betsy's killer, if it's not the same person as who threatened my mother, has to be second. After all, we won't be able to do Betsy any good at this point, but I have a feeling that if we're quick enough, and good enough, we might be able to stop something very bad from happening to my mother."

"Then let's be quick *and* good," Grace agreed with a firm nod.

"That's the plan," I replied.

As we passed the hospital, I couldn't help but remember rushing there the day before, afraid of what I was going to find. It had been Betsy, not Momma, dead there, but it had still managed to give me the fright of my life.

I was going to make sure that my mother's fate didn't match Betsy's or die trying to protect her myself.

"Did you see that?" I asked Grace as I parked in front of Gerard Mince's office.

"The SUV's gone, and there's a truck parked there instead. I wonder why he didn't come to work in the same vehicle we saw here yesterday?"

"Maybe he *couldn't* drive it, since the front fender was dented from hitting Betsy Wilkes," I said.

"It's possible. Should we come right out and ask him?"

"Yes, but let's save that question for the end. I doubt he'll be happy about answering it."

"I can do that," Grace said. "Come on, Suzanne. Let's go tackle the bear in his lair."

"Shouldn't that be a den?" I asked her. "Do bears have lairs?"

"They do if it's cold outside," Grace said with a grin. "After all, a bear sweater just isn't enough sometimes, and they need lots and lots of lairs if they're going to stay warm."

I grinned. "Enough with the wordplay. Let's save our cleverness for our suspect."

I was about to open the door when it opened for me. A large, heavyset man with a pair of the most unfortunate bushy eyebrows I'd ever seen in my life looked unhappy to find us on his doorstep. I decided to make a preemptive strike. "Mr. Mince, I'd love a moment of your time."

"Save it," he said abruptly. "I know who you are."

"Okay, I was about to introduce myself, but I'm glad that's not going to be necessary," I said with a smile I didn't feel.

"How about me? Care to take a guess as to who I might be?" Grace asked him with a slight grin of her own.

"I don't know, and frankly, if you're keeping company with Dorothea Hart's daughter, I don't care. Now get out of my way. I don't want to be late."

"Then we'll make it quick," I said as I stood my ground. I wasn't about to let this gruff man brush us off, at least not so easily.

"Shouldn't you be making cookies at your store instead of bothering me?" he asked me with a scowl.

"It's donuts, thank you very much, and my second team is working the shop today so we could come here and talk to you about the threat my mother got yesterday morning."

"I don't know what you're talking about," he said. Was there a hint of hesitation before he did, though? I wondered.

"Let me refresh your memory. It said, *I know what you did, and you aren't going to get away with it.* Sound familiar?"

"No, I can't say that it does," he said as he tried to sidestep around me. Grace was there waiting for him, though. "What's this got to do with me?"

"We heard you were pretty upset when she took your legs out from under you on that last business deal," I said sweetly. "It must have been upsetting to say the least."

He barked out a laugh. "Did she put you up to this? I suppose she said she got the better of me. Well, I was having second thoughts about going ahead with the project because of one of my co-investors, so she actually did me a favor. That place is a dog, and she's going to get burned buying it."

"Funny, but that's not the way Cordelia Bush described your behavior," I said.

"You spoke with Cordelia? Listen, I didn't write that note, but even if I did, so what? There's nothing illegal about leaving someone a note."

"There is if you're threatening them," I said, though I wasn't at all sure if it was true, strictly speaking.

"It doesn't sound like a threat to me."

"Really?" Grace asked a little sternly. "What would you call it, then?"

"An observation," he answered. "Now if you'll excuse me, I've had enough of your questions for one day." This time he bulled forward, and I knew we were going to lose him soon. After all, he was under no obligation to answer any of our questions. It wasn't like we had any legal means to get him to cooperate with our investigation. We had to rely on craftiness and guile. Fortunately, Grace and I had an ample supply of each.

"Hey, Gerard, where's the fancy dark SUV you were driving yesterday?" I asked him as he reached for the door handle of his truck.

"You didn't have an accident in it, did you?" Grace followed up.

"That's none of your business," he said. "Now I've got to get to an auction."

He got into his truck and drove quickly out of the parking lot.

"Quick! Get in the Jeep," I told Grace as I did as I'd instructed her to do.

"Are we going to follow him?" she asked as she buckled her seat belt.

"No, we're going to his house to see if his car killed Betsy Wilkes."

"How are we going to manage that?" Grace asked me as I started driving. "Do we even know where he lives?"

"I found it online yesterday," I admitted. "I figured if he wasn't at his office today, we might be able to rouse him out of bed and ask him our questions there."

"This is so much better," Grace said. "Do you honestly think he'd leave his car sitting in the driveway if he used it to kill someone?"

"No, it's probably in his garage, but that doesn't necessarily have to stop us."

Grace smiled and rubbed her hands together. "Finally, a game plan I can sink my teeth into. You know me. There's nothing like a little breaking and entering to start my day."

"It's nearly eleven, our day's been going on for some time, and we're not going to break into anything if we can help it," I told her.

"Fine, we'll do it your way," she said a little grumpily. "How are we supposed to find out about his car if we aren't going to break into his garage, though?"

"It's got windows, so we can peek inside," I said.

"How could you possibly know that?"

"Online again. I found a photo of his place there."

"What did we do before there was an Internet?" she asked me.

"In some ways, I think things were better then, but at least for this, I'm glad we have access to it," I admitted.

"Suzanne, you're such a Luddite sometimes," she said with a grin.

"That's not true. I just think there's way too much information out there for everyone to see. Strike that. There's too much *noise*. Everyone sounds so convincing in their anonymity that they're right and the rest of us are just bumbling idiots stumbling around in the dark. What we don't realize is that most of the self-appointed 'authorities' that sound so convincing are just lonely people sitting around in their pajamas, laughing and watching the world burn around them."

"That's kind of a dark way of looking at modern technology, isn't it?" Grace asked. "It does a great deal of good, too."

"I don't always feel so strongly about it, but you caught me in a bad moment. While I was online after Momma was threatened, I searched her name, and then I checked Donut Hearts out on a lark. I *hated* what I read. It turns out that there are some anonymous trolls who seem to take great delight in trying to tear down my life's work."

"That's terrible," she agreed. "Do you have any idea who would say such bad things about your donut shop?"

"No, that's the problem. They have perfect immunity and anonymity. It could be someone who's a regular customer of mine, or a complete stranger living halfway around the world."

"It could even be a criminal you helped put away exacting a little revenge from their jail cell," Grace added softly.

"Somehow that prospect is even scarier," I said. "Do convicts really have access to the Internet while they're in jail?"

"You don't want to know. Take my advice and don't search for it online. The thing is, even if they *aren't* posting from their prison accounts, how hard would it be to smuggle a cell phone into jail? With one of those, the world is a pretty small place, but I wouldn't let the negative comments worry me if I were you, since there's nothing you can do about it, anyway."

"I'll do my best not to let it get to me, but I can't promise anything," I said. "We're here," I added as we pulled up in front of a stately home with large white columns out front and a well-manicured lawn spreading over what had to be at least an acre of grass. The garage was just as I'd seen it represented online, and there were two sets of windows along the front of the space so that it matched the architecture of the rest of the house.

With any luck, we'd be able to confirm or refute the fact that Gerard Mince was indeed our killer.

Chapter 12

"ARE THOSE REAL CURTAINS?" Grace asked as we neared the windows of the garage.

"It looks like it to me," I said. "The only chance we have of seeing anything is to walk through the mulch and the bushes and see if there isn't a gap in the material somewhere we can see through."

"You realize that we're going to be kind of obvious if someone happens to drive by, or even glance out their window, don't you?"

I looked around. "We have a few things going for us. At this time of day, most of the folks around here are probably off at work so they can afford such nice houses to begin with. Two, it's a cul-de-sac, so there are only three houses that look out onto where we are right now. I don't know. I like our odds."

"Then let's be brazen and go for it," Grace answered with a smile.

We walked down the sidewalk that led to the garage, whose door was on the side of the house and not in front, and we neared the first window.

There was absolutely no gap at all in the curtains, and they were substantial enough to block our view completely.

"Let's try the other one," I suggested.

"If this window doesn't show anything, there are always the windows in back," she said.

"Maybe we should check there first," I answered. "Chances are there aren't any curtains or blinds back there at all."

We left the mulched area and walked around the large double garage doors. They were in the shape of carriage doors of old, even including some hardware hinges that had obviously been added later. That was up close, though. From a distance, they looked like they were in perfect working order. I didn't even have a carport at the cottage, let alone a garage with its own dedicated door.

"Should we just leave the Jeep parked in the driveway like that?" Grace asked as she glanced back.

"We won't be here long, and if anybody does see it, they'll just think that Gerard has company."

Together, we walked around to the back, and I saw that Grace had been right.

There was nothing blocking the windows to the garage on the back side of the house.

There was a vehicle inside, but there was also a problem.

It was clear that a tarp covered the SUV from front to back.

If we were going to see if any damage had been done to Gerard Mince's personal car, we were going to have to break into the garage to find out.

I checked the first window, trying to force it open with my palms pressed flat against it.

"What are you doing, Suzanne?"

"I'm not keen on breaking, but I'd love to enter," I admitted as I tried to force the window open.

It wouldn't budge.

"Now you're talking," Grace said as she tried the other garage window in back.

"No luck," she said as she frowned. "Hey, how about using one of these landscaping pavers?"

"What for?" I asked, though I suspected exactly what she was suggesting.

"Well, if I should pick one up and it happened to slip out of my hands and go through the glass, is that really such a bad thing? You said it yourself. Nobody's around."

"Probably not, but that doesn't mean that he doesn't have an alarm system."

She peeked inside at the window frame. "I don't see any contacts on the glass. I don't think everyone wires their garages, just their houses. We should be fine."

"There are too many variables," I said. "Don't forget, we don't *think* anybody else is around, but we don't know that for sure. Besides, what if it *is* wired? We're going to have to hightail it out of here if we break in and an alarm goes off. And what if we *do* find the front fender dented in from the impact of killing Betsy Wilkes? We can't exactly call the police and tell them what we've discovered."

"So we're just giving up?" she asked me.

"I didn't say that," I answered as I started back toward the garage doors.

Once we were there, I reached down and tried to pull up on each in turn. Maybe we could get in that way.

We couldn't.

Then I spotted something mounted to the doorframe.

"Is that what I think it is?" I asked her as I flipped up the cover.

"It's a keypad," Grace said, "but without the code, we'll never get in."

I studied the numbers anyway, and I saw that only the 8 and the 2 had any smudges on them at all. "We're in luck. It appears Gerard has a limited imagination. How many combinations can there be of eights and twos?"

"I don't know, but I bet it's more than the three or four tries we get before the system activates," she said.

"You're thinking of alarms again, not keyless entries," I said. "We can stand out here all day if we have to and it won't make a bit of difference."

"I don't know about that," Grace said as she started punching eights and twos randomly.

"Fingerprints!" I warned her. "You don't want to leave any on the pad, in case he finds out we've been here."

"No worries," she said. "The pad will be easy enough to wipe off once we crack the code."

"We can't just punch numbers in randomly," I told her. "We need a system."

As I said it, the door began to lift. Grace grinned at me as she wiped away her own prints, and most of the smudges we'd found. "8282. Wow, that was easier than I thought it was going to be."

"Okay, it appears your system worked just fine," I apologized.

"What can I say? I got lucky."

Once the door was open, I headed straight for the car and lifted up one corner of the cover on it.

It was the rear end of the vehicle, and there wasn't a mark anywhere on it.

Grace moved around and did the same in the front.

"Suzanne, you need to come see this," she said as she pulled out her phone and took a picture of it.

As I walked around the car, I felt a chill.

The front left bumper was dented in, and someone had obviously made an effort to clean off whatever they'd hit.

I was about to reach for my own phone when I heard an ominous voice behind us.

"What do you two think you're doing in my garage?"

It appeared that we hadn't been as invisible as we'd hoped after all.

Chapter 13

"THE DOOR WAS OPEN WHEN we got here," Grace lied quickly.

"That's not true, and we all know it. I should call the police on you."

"Yes, do that, please," I said. "I'll take a little trespassing over what they're going to charge you with. Hit-and-run murder is a pretty serious charge."

"I hit a tree," Gerard protested. "I doubt the authorities are going to press charges for doing that. It was foggy last night, and I missed the cutoff on a back road as I was coming home. I was lost in the fog, and I still honestly have no idea where it happened."

"So you can't prove anything," I said. "Still, you did a good job cleaning it up, but I'm willing to bet that you didn't get every last trace of whatever you hit off of it."

"That's it. I've had enough of this insanity." He pulled out his cell phone and dialed 911. "Hello? I'd like to report a break-in at my home. Yes, they're still here. Hurry, please, there's no telling what they might do." He smiled a little maliciously after he added the last bit and ended the call. "That should get them here in a hurry."

I couldn't believe that he'd actually had the nerve to call the police. Was it possible that he was telling the truth about hitting a tree and not Betsy Wilkes? Or was he that confident that he had removed every last trace of evidence of the crime?

The flashing lights and sirens announced that we were about to be visited by the police.

With his gun drawn, a police officer barely in his twenties got out of his car and shouted at all three of us. "Get down on the ground! Now!"

"I'm the one who called you," Gerard announced calmly. "I'm not getting down anywhere."

"Mister, I don't know *who* you are, but if you don't do exactly as I tell you, I'll put you down myself."

It had almost been worth getting caught just to see the expression on Gerard Mince's face. Grace and I dropped right where we were, and Gerard joined us a few seconds later, albeit reluctantly.

He was still blustering, though prone now, about his innocence when another squad car pulled up. This one said Chief of Police on the side of it, and an unfamiliar woman in uniform joined us. "What's going on, Andrews?"

"When I responded to a 911 call, I found them inside."

"So you ordered *all* of them to the ground?" she asked, a hint of displeasure in her voice. "Didn't you even try to ascertain if one of them might actually live here?"

"That's what I've been trying to tell him. I do," Gerard sputtered as he glared at Officer Andrews.

"I was about to check IDs when you showed up, Chief," he explained in lieu of an apology.

Instead of saying anything, she just shook her head. "Go on, get back out on patrol."

He looked shocked by the order. "I should stay and give you backup, Chief," he insisted.

She looked us over quickly before replying, "I believe I'll be all right. Go."

The last word was barked out as a severe order, and there was no doubt who was in charge.

Once the officer was gone, she turned to Gerard. "Why don't you stand up slowly and reach for your wallet? I need to see some identification."

He did as he was told, and after she confirmed the fact that the address listed on his driver's license was the same as where we were standing, she said, "Thank you, Mr. Mince. Sorry for the confusion, but you can't be too careful."

"May we stand as well?" Grace asked.

"In a second," she answered before turning back to Gerard. "Would you mind telling me what's going on here?"

"One of my neighbors called to tell me that someone was breaking into my house," he said. "When I got here, I found the two of them skulking around inside my garage, where they had no right to be."

"We were hardly skulking," I protested, and a lie suddenly occurred to me. "We spoke with Mr. Mince earlier, and we wanted to follow up with him about something. The garage door was open when we arrived, and we thought he might be inside. That's when he showed up and called you."

Grace nodded as though I'd just told the complete and utter truth.

"Do you know these women?" the police chief asked. "I haven't seen them around Maple Hollow, but then again, I've only been in town a few weeks."

That explained why she was unfamiliar to me.

Gerard Mince blustered, "Just because I know them doesn't mean that they weren't here illegally! Now I demand that you arrest them immediately!"

"Are you sure you want me to do that?" she asked him calmly.

"You women are all alike, aren't you?" he asked with a sneer. "I should have known you'd believe them over me. After all, I've committed the crime of being a successful white man."

The police chief pursed her lips for a moment before she spoke, but it was clear that Gerard Mince's outburst had angered her. Instead of saying anything to him immediately, she looked down at us and said, "Ladies, you can get up now. I'd like to see some identification from you too, please, if you don't mind."

We both pulled out our drivers' licenses without saying a word. She took them each in turn and wrote down the pertinent information on them before handing them back to us. As she gave me mine back, she asked, "You're not related to Jake Bishop by any chance, are you?"

"He's my husband. Why, do you know him?" I asked.

"We've met. He's a good cop."

"He used to be," I corrected her. "He's consulting now."

"That's right, I heard that he'd left the force," she replied.

Gerard was beside himself. "You're letting them go, aren't you? I can't believe it!"

"Sir, it's your word against theirs. The garage door may or may not have been open when they arrived. Look around. Was *anything* taken?"

"Not that I can see," he agreed reluctantly.

"Then I suggest you drop it," she ordered.

"What about his front left fender?" I asked her.

"What about it?"

"A woman in April Springs was run over yesterday afternoon, and whoever did it fled the scene in an SUV matching his vehicle. His fender is dented in, and he claimed it was because he hit a tree last night in the fog, though he has no idea where it might have been."

She frowned as she approached the car. We'd pulled up the cover, but Gerard had tugged it back down as soon as he'd arrived.

As the chief started toward it, Mince said, "You're going to need a warrant to look at that. I might not be able to get these two criminals charged, but I'll be dipped in manure if I'm going to stand here and let you run roughshod over me. Now I'd like to ask you all to leave right now."

The police chief looked at him for a moment, and then she turned to us. "Ladies, let's do as he wishes and go."

Once we were outside, the garage door closed, cutting us off from Gerard Mince.

"Thanks, Chief," I said gratefully.

"You should thank your husband. The door was just standing open, huh? If that was the case, then why was the cover for the remote entry still open? How did you know the code? No, never mind. I don't want to know."

Grace must have forgotten to close it again, and I'd been too preoccupied with the car to notice. "Maybe he leaves it open all of the time," I suggested.

"Maybe," she said, though it was clear she didn't believe any more than he did that we'd just waltzed right into an already open garage.

"Are you going to get a warrant to search his garage?" I asked her.

"On what grounds?"

"Call April Springs. Not only can Chief Grant vouch for us, but he can tell you what happened to Betsy Wilkes."

"I suppose you know this chief pretty well," the new Maple Hollow chief of police said.

"I should," Grace said. "After all, he's sort of my fiancé."

The chief looked puzzled by Grace's statement. "How can you 'sort of' be engaged to him?"

"He's asked; I just haven't answered yet," she admitted.

The chief shook her head. "Listen, do me a favor. From now on, don't go where you're not welcome, whether the door is already open or not when you get there, at least not in Maple Hollow."

"We'll do our best not to," I said, "but if we went only where we were welcome, Grace and I would stay home a lot."

That got the ghost of a smile before she wiped it away. "Tell your husband Officer Liddy Holmes said hello."

"I will," I promised, "and thanks again."

"What, for not arresting you? There's no way those charges would stick, and I hate wasting my time on things that don't matter. Just don't make a habit of it, okay?"

"Okay," I agreed.

Once we were back in the Jeep and heading toward April Springs again, Grace pulled out her cell phone.

"Who are you calling now?" I asked her.

"It doesn't matter, because it's busy," she said with a frown.

"That doesn't answer my question," I said.

Instead of answering me, she hit redial a few times, and when it finally started ringing, she put it on speaker, and I heard Chief Grant answer.

"Hey, it's me," Grace said.

"I was wondering how long it would take you to call. I just got off the phone with the new police chief of Maple Hollow. It was an uncomfortable conversation having to vouch for my...er...girlfriend like that. Was that door really already open when you got there?"

"It was open when we walked through it," she said. "Wow, she didn't waste any time calling you, did she?"

"What, did you think she'd dawdle before she checked your story out with me?" the chief asked her.

"I'm not surprised that she's thorough, but did she tell you what we found in Gerard Mince's garage? He has a dinged front fender, Stephen. He killed Betsy Wilkes."

"Hang on a second. That's a pretty strong accusation. Where's your proof? He didn't admit to doing it, did he?"

"He said he hit a tree in the fog last night," I interjected. "Hey, Chief, it's Suzanne."

"Hello," he said. "What motive could Gerard Mince possibly have for running Betsy down?"

"He thought she was my mother," I explained. "It's obvious, isn't it?"

"Maybe to you, but it's not enough for me to get a search warrant," he replied.

"Are you honestly going to just ignore it and hope it goes away? She died in your arms, Stephen," Grace said, clearly distraught by his statement.

"Do you think you need to remind me of that?" he asked her icily.

"I'm sorry," Grace interjected quickly. "That was the wrong thing to say."

"Yes, it was," he said coldly. "I said I couldn't get a warrant, but that doesn't mean that I'm going to let it go, either. I have constraints about what I can and cannot do in the course of an investigation, unlike the two of you. This inquiry will be handled strictly by the book. Now, if you two could stay out of trouble for at least the next two days, I'd greatly appreciate it."

As Grace started to apologize again, he hung up on us.

Chapter 14

"I'M SORRY ABOUT THAT," I said into the growing silence of the Jeep.

"It's not your fault," Grace answered quickly.

"In a way it was. Don't forget, it was my idea to go inside the garage in the first place," I reminded her.

"It wasn't as though you had to twist my arm, Suzanne. I was ready to throw a concrete paver through the window, remember?" she asked me with a grin. "He'll be okay. He just needs to cool off a little bit."

"I hope you're right," I said. "So, what do you think? Have we found Betsy's killer?"

"It seems clear enough, doesn't it? Then again, he could have been telling us the truth. It *was* foggy last night."

"How could you possibly know that? You were in April Springs, weren't you?"

"I was, but I used the demon Internet to find out," she answered with a slight smile as she wiggled her phone at me.

"I didn't mean it that way, and you know it," I replied.

"I know. I don't blame you for being upset. Someone attacked your baby."

"I'll get over it," I admitted.

"And so will Stephen," she replied. "I still think we need to keep going forward with our investigations. If it turns out that Gerard did run Betsy over, Stephen and Chief Holmes will uncover the truth."

"Do you think they'll keep digging into it?" I asked her.

"You saw the look in her eyes. What do you think? I know you've seen that same expression in Jake's gaze, and I've certainly seen it enough in Stephen's to realize what it means. She's not going to rest until she finds out if Gerard Mince killed Betsy or not. In the meantime though, we need to speak with Ellie Westmore again."

"What can we ask her today that we didn't ask her yesterday?" I asked Grace.

"We'll think of something. That's not the real reason I want to see her."

"You want to get a look at her car, don't you?"

"Don't you?" she asked me.

"You know I do, and we shouldn't have to get a warrant to see it. Unlike Gerard Mince, Ellie has a carport in back of her house. Anyone, even the two of us, can just walk back there without breaking or entering anything."

"Even if she catches us in the act and claims that we're trespassing, I can't imagine Ellie Westmore calling the police on us, but if she does, I've got connections with the chief," Grace added. "At least I think I still do."

"I'm sure you two are good," I said, wishing fervently that it was true.

"I hope so," she said.

We'd just passed the hospital and were nearly back into town when my cell phone rang. As I put it on speaker, I heard a familiar voice chide me, "Suzanne, I can't believe you did something so incredibly *irresponsible*." There was no mistaking the scolding tone of my mother's voice.

"How did you hear about that already?" I asked, going into full-on defense mode. I put a finger to my lips for Grace to stay silent. I didn't want Momma to think that we were ganging up on her. "It happened less than an hour ago."

The line went silent for a moment, and then she asked, "What are you talking about?"

"Nothing. Why? What are *you* talking about?" It wasn't the most adult way to blunt her question, but sometimes I reverted to my teenaged self when it came to dealing with accusations from my mother.

"Suzanne Hart, what have you two been up to now?"

"Grace and I had a little run-in with Gerard Mince at his house," I admitted. After all, there was no reason to lie about it. Given the way gossip traveled around our part of North Carolina, I was sure she'd hear an exaggerated version of the incident soon enough, so she might as well hear my particular spin on what had happened first.

"What kind of run-in?" she asked sharply.

"We were in his garage looking at his car, and he came home and found us there." I'd almost said caught instead of found, but I wasn't sure that my choice of words made any difference.

"You were trespassing *and* breaking and entering? What were you two thinking?"

"We were thinking that we might try to save your life from another attempt on it," I said, snapping a bit more than I should have. "Besides, we didn't break anything."

"I suppose the garage door was just standing wide open for you to waltz through?"

"Hey, anybody who uses 8282 as a security code and punches it in with dirty fingers *deserves* to get his garage violated," I said.

Momma sighed a bit, and I could swear I heard her stifle a laugh. "Why were you in his garage in the first place, Suzanne?"

"Yesterday at his office we saw that he was driving a car that turned out to match the description of the vehicle that hit Betsy," I explained. "When we got to his office today, he was driving his work truck, so naturally we were suspicious about what might have happened to his usual vehicle."

After a pause, she asked, "And what did you find?"

"The car was covered in some kind of tarp, and when we lifted the edge of it, we found the front fender dented," I said.

"No. I can't believe it. Did you confront him about it when he found you two lurking in his garage?"

"We weren't exactly lurking," I corrected her. "He said he hit a tree in some fog last night. We wanted to show the police chief when she showed up, but he'd already pulled the tarp back down, and she couldn't look at it without a warrant, or probable cause, or something like that," I said, throwing out expressions from the latest mystery novel I was reading. My book club might have been on hiatus, but that didn't stop me from reading in my off moments, as rare as those might have been.

"The *chief of police* was there?" she asked, sounding more incredulous with each twist and turn the conversation took.

"It's okay, Momma. No one got arrested. I still can't believe Gerard called the cops on us."

"It doesn't sound like something a man guilty of murder would do though, does it?" Momma asked me.

"No, not really," I agreed. "Could he really be that brazen if he killed Betsy yesterday?"

"With that man, it's difficult to say," Momma said. "At least you're both not in jail. I suppose that's something."

"Hey, what did you call me about if it wasn't about the garage?" I asked her.

"Oh, yes. That's right. Why did you call my husband?"

It was my turn to be surprised. "What? I never called Phillip."

"Did you speak with Jake about what was going on last night?" Momma asked me.

"I did," I freely admitted. "He asked me what I was up to, and I told him."

"And he called Phillip the moment you hung up, I'll wager. Well, he's on his way home even as we speak. He should be here in a few hours."

"Jake is coming back?" I asked, confused by her statement.

"No, Phillip is. Keep up, Suzanne. The entire point of this trip was to allow him some peace to come to terms with what's been happening to him lately, and now that's all been ruined."

"Momma, to be fair, if the roles had been reversed, you would have told Phillip, and I'd bet good money that his next call would have been to Jake. We have to face the fact that our husbands love us. It's a heavy burden to carry at times, but I'm afraid that it's our lot in life. Look at it the other way. If you thought there was the slightest chance that *he* were in trouble, wouldn't *you* drop everything and come running, no matter what?"

Momma took a moment to process that, and then she laughed softly. "You're right. I apologize. I overreacted."

"It's okay. You're only human, after all," I said.

"As are you. Your lapse in judgment today is proof enough of that. So, are you focusing solely on Gerard Mince now? I wouldn't suggest it, at least not if I were you. It's too bold a move calling in law enforcement when the murder weapon was sitting just a few feet away."

"You know, you might be right," I said, feeling a lot less confident about my views about Gerard as the killer. "We're going to keep digging."

"What's next, or should I say whom?"

"You can say whom if you want, but it's always going to be 'who' for me," I said. "I don't care if it's grammatically correct or not, 'whom' sounds stuffy to me."

"I want a name, Suzanne."

"We're going to speak with Ellie Westmore again, and while we're there, we're going to take a peek at her car," I said.

"That's not a bad idea," she said.

"Momma, you aren't planning on joining us there, are you?" I asked. "Because if you are, we've already discussed it, and it's still a bad idea."

"I might be tempted, but I have a dozen things to wrap up before my husband comes home," she said. "I really wish that Jake hadn't called him." Was there a hint of relief in her voice that he'd done it anyway, though?

"Sorry, but if you have a problem with my husband, you're going to need to take it up with him. What can I say? We all love you, and we all want to protect you. For that I will not apologize, not now, not ever."

"I love you too, Suzanne," Momma said. "And you as well, Grace," she added.

"How did you know I was listening in?" Grace asked her, speaking for the first time.

Momma laughed. "Please. The two of you are so transparent, at least to me, that I can predict your moves before you even make them."

"You didn't know about the garage though, did you?" I asked with a hint of laughter in my voice.

"No, sometimes you manage to surprise even me. I'm sure I'll be speaking with you both later. Good-bye for now."

After we said our own good-byes, I ended the call.

"Your mother is one sharp cookie, isn't she?" Grace observed.

"I didn't get away with anything as a kid, but I thought I'd at least be able to fool her every now and then as an adult."

"Sorry, but I don't think that's going to happen," she said. As we drove past the bank, Grace said, "Pull over, Suzanne."

I did as she asked without question, and then I saw the woman she was pointing at.

Evidently Ellie Westmore had decided to leave her car at home today and walk.

I wondered if she had a motivating reason to do that, and I was certainly going to ask her as soon as I could.

"Are you walking today?" I asked Ellie as we approached her.

"Why not? After all, it's a beautiful day."

I looked up at the sky. It was overcast, a bit chilly, and spitting rain. I enjoyed that kind of weather, but then again, I wouldn't choose it as a day to walk into town, a trek that had to be a good three miles from her house each way.

"You're not having car troubles, are you?" Grace asked her.

"No, my car's just fine," she said. "If you stopped to offer me a ride in that Jeep of yours, I'll pass. I never trusted those things."

"What's wrong with my vehicle?" I asked. I was a bit possessive of it, though I knew firsthand that it wasn't perfect.

But it was perfect for me.

"Nothing," she amended quickly, no doubt seeing me bristle. "I used to date a gentleman with one a very long time ago, and it was constantly breaking down on him."

"I assure you that mine will get you wherever you need to go," I said.

"Where I need to go is the grocery store," she said, "and I'm fine doing it on two feet."

"Are you saying that you're going to lug a bunch of groceries home in the rain instead of taking your car?" I asked her.

"Honestly, I don't see that it's really any of your business, Suzanne," she said a bit abruptly. "Now if you'll excuse me, I need to be on my way."

"What about our meeting at eleven, the one you were so insistent on having?" I asked her.

"I've changed my mind. It was nothing important."

As she started to go, Grace said, "I have to hand it to you, ma'am. It's really brave of you to be out walking, especially today."

"Why, because of the weather? I'm not a delicate little flower, and I'm certainly not afraid of getting a little wet."

"I wasn't talking about the weather," Grace said. "I meant the fact that yesterday someone ran Betsy Wilkes down while she was out on a walk, too."

Ellie didn't pause, she didn't even turn around.

She just kept walking away from us.

"Let's go check something out while we have the chance," I said once we were back in the Jeep.

"Did you see that? She couldn't even look at us after I mentioned Betsy's name. Suzanne, maybe she had something to do with that after all."

"I don't know if she did or she didn't, but there's something I want to see."

"Where are we going?" she asked me.

"Where we talked about going before. We're going to go check out Ellie's car. I just realized that I don't know what she drives these days."

We got to her place, and at least this time, we knew that there was no danger of her catching us there. As I'd told Grace earlier, Ellie had a carport in back of her house, not a full garage, so it wouldn't be too difficult checking out her car.

The carport was large enough for two vehicles, but there was just one parked there at the moment, though there were stains and some dirt on the unoccupied section as well. Beside the vehicle, there was an assortment of gardening tools hung up on the side wall, everything from large pruning shears to saws to an old-fashioned scythe, but the car was really all that mattered at the moment.

It was a small red Toyota Yaris, hardly something anyone would mistake for a dark SUV, and besides that, there wasn't a mark on it.

Apparently Ellie Westmore wasn't the killer, at least not using that vehicle.

"Well, that was a big dead end," Grace said. "What should we do now?"

I was about to answer when my stomach grumbled. "Are you hungry?"

"I could eat," she said with a smile. "What did you have in mind?"

"How about the Boxcar Grill again?" I suggested. "I don't know about you, but I'm craving a burger and fries."

"Then we should indulge that craving by all means," she replied.

When we got there though, the parking lot was jammed. "What is Trish doing, giving food away today?" I asked as I searched for a spot to park. "Should we even bother going in?"

"Where else are we going to eat? You mentioned a burger and fries, and now that's the only thing I can think of."

I glanced across the street. "Donut Hearts is closed for the day. Let's park over there and walk across the street," I suggested.

"Sounds good to me. I can build up my appetite that way."

After I got out, I glanced up the tracks toward the grill. "How many laps are you thinking about doing before we eat?"

"Come on, don't be such a sissy," she said with a laugh.

I noticed that I'd picked up a bit of oil on one of my tennis shoes somewhere. As I scraped it on the grass, I said, "I hate chewing gum, oil, and dog poo on my shoes."

"I don't like to take showers in thunderstorms, and I hate smooth peanut butter," Grace said with a smile as I finished wiping my shoe.

"What does any of that have to do with anything?" I asked her. She was my best friend, and yet she still managed to exasperate me on occasion. I took a bit of solace from the fact that I did the same to her at times.

"I thought we were just listing things we didn't like," she said with a grin. "Don't be such a baby. Most of it came off. Now let's go grab something tasty. I'm in the mood for a bit of decadence."

"Then we're going to the right place," I told her. "Who knows? Maybe we'll even have room for a bit of dessert."

"If we don't, I'll be severely disappointed with both of us," Grace replied with a grin.

Chapter 15

"SORRY WE'RE SO JAMMED," Trish said with a frown the moment we walked through the door. It looked as though we weren't even going to get our main courses, let alone desserts.

"What's going on?" I asked her.

"I have no idea. Sometimes we can barely fill the place up this time of day, and others, everybody decides all at once to have lunch out. Do you want me to evict somebody for you?"

I was about to decline her offer when I saw the mayor wave at us from his table. "It looks like we're in luck. We're sitting with George."

"Good," Trish said as she rang up someone's bill. "I'll be over there shortly to take your orders."

We said a few hellos as we walked toward the mayor's table, and as we neared it, he stood and smiled. "Care to join me, ladies?"

"It's either that or we sit on the floor," I said with a grin.

"Well, I've had more gracious acceptances to my invitations in the past, but I'll take it."

"Thanks for letting us sit with you, Mr. Mayor," Grace said as she took a chair.

"Now see, that wasn't so hard, was it, Suzanne? You could be more like your compatriot here, you know."

"I could, but what fun would that be?" I asked as I took a seat myself. "How are you doing, my friend?"

"I'm fine," he said a bit blandly.

"Really? Fine? You don't look fine."

"Suzanne," Grace said. "Be nice."

"I am," I said without looking away from the mayor. "What's going on?"

"What do you think? I've got woman problems yet again," he said with a frown.

"It's your own fault. You're the mayor around here, and that makes you a desirable date, at least in some women's eyes."

"Maybe so, but they aren't the women that *I'm* interested in," he said with a sigh.

"Do you have someone in particular in mind?" Grace asked him as Trish approached.

"I took the liberty of ordering two sweet teas for you," she said as she deposited them in front of us. After topping George's glass off, she asked, "What will it be?"

"Two burgers and fries. You know the way we like them," I told her.

"Yours has extra sardines, and Grace likes lots and lots of horseradish. Got it," she answered with a grin.

I glanced over at George as Trish left, and a light bulb went off in my mind. "Trish? Seriously?" I asked him.

"What?" he asked as he glanced at me. "What are you talking about?"

"*Trish* is the woman you're interested in?" I asked him.

"Keep your voice down, would you?" he hissed at me. "I know she's young enough to be my daughter, but there's something about her that I like. She's sassy, you know?"

"Oh, I know," I said softly. "You should ask her out."

"What, and look like a fool? I know what people would say. I'm twenty years her senior, probably closer to thirty. I won't have people laughing at me behind my back," he said.

"What do you care what they say or think?" I asked him. "You both deserve to be happy, and if that means that it's together, let the tongues wag all they like. It's not like she'd be going out with you for your money, anyway, because you don't have any," I added with a grin.

He chuckled slightly. "That much is true enough. It's just a crazy thought. I don't know what we'd talk about. We're from two different generations. I just wish I could meet someone closer to my own age who isn't so stuffy, you know?" He lowered his voice so softly that I barely heard the next thing he had to say. "I'm just lonely, I guess."

"Well, we can't have that," I said. "I still think that you should ask Trish out."

"No, that's not going to happen," he said firmly, and I knew my friend well enough to realize that he meant it.

"Okay, then, we'll just find you someone more age appropriate with the same qualities you like in her," Grace chimed in.

"Hang on a second. I don't need you two matchmaking on my behalf," George said abruptly.

"We'd never do that," I said with mock innocence.

"Of course not," Grace chimed in with a grin that matched my own.

"I mean it," George said severely. "I don't want anyone's help."

"Suit yourself," I said, though that didn't mean that I wouldn't start thinking about his dilemma. I knew April Springs wasn't that big, but he didn't have to narrow his focus to just our area. If he was insistent on finding someone closer to his age, we might have to spread our nets out a little bit further than the town limits sign, but would that be such a bad thing? Maybe the reason George hadn't been with anyone for a while was because he was narrowing his dating pool too much.

Trish brought our burgers, thankfully without sardines and horseradish, though I wouldn't have put it past her to do so as a joke. As she placed our platters in front of us, I asked her, "Trish, how's your love life been recently?"

"Actually, I've started seeing two different guys, and I've never been happier," she answered.

I nearly dropped the catsup bottle I was about to use. "When did this happen? How did you meet two guys at once?"

"They were together at the time," she said. "I was at the grocery store, and I stumbled across them. One's named Ben, and the other one is Jerry."

"At least they aren't Jim Beam and Johnny Walker," Grace said, naming two hard liquors.

"No, the ice cream guys are a lot more my speed," she said. "Honestly, I've given up dating. There's just no one all that interesting to me around here."

"What do you like in a man?" Grace asked her before she took the first bite of her burger.

George's face was growing noticeably redder and redder by the minute, but I don't think Trish even noticed. "Let's see, he's got to be young and vigorous, but not too young, you know? I like to take hikes sometimes, but then again, I love a good movie every now and then. Most of all, I guess he has to get my sense of humor. You'd be amazed at how many men don't appreciate my particular wit."

"I would be," I said. "How old are you willing to go?"

George kicked me under the table, but I did my best not to flinch.

"I don't know. Maybe forty?" she asked. "I'm not sure if I could go much older than that. Why the sudden interest in my love life, ladies?"

"We care about you, and we want you to be happy," I said in all sincerity.

"I appreciate that, but honestly, I'm enjoying a little Trish time at the moment, so don't get any ideas and try to set me up with some stranger."

"Never," Grace said with a straight face.

"We wouldn't dream of it," I added.

Once she was gone, George frowned at each of us in turn. "You two think you're cute, don't you?"

"Grace is the adorable one," I said. "I'm not sure I qualify as cute."

"Come on, I've *always* described you that way," she countered.

We both looked at George, and then we gave him identical grins.

He wanted to be angry, we could see it in his eyes, but he just couldn't bring himself to hold onto it. Finally, he laughed, and we joined in as well.

"At least now I know that Trish isn't interested in an old goat like me, so I can stop pining away for her," he replied.

"Were you really pining?" I asked him, dead serious.

"No, not really, but it's good to know that she isn't interested. Don't you two worry about me. I'll figure it out."

"I know you will, and for what it's worth," I said as I patted his hand gently, "when you do find whoever it is you're looking for, she'll be worth the wait."

"How can you be so sure of that?" he asked me.

"Call it a feeling," I said.

George shook his head, but he was still smiling. "Then I won't worry about it anymore. After all, Suzanne's got a feeling, so what more do I need?"

"Exactly," I said as I took a bite of burger. Hilda was on her game back in the kitchen. I wasn't sure what kind of seasoning she used, but her burgers just tasted better than any of the others I got out. Maybe it was the love she put into her cooking, but I had a hunch it was something a little more technical. I knew better than to ask her what kind of spices and seasonings she used. She protected that information as though it were a state secret.

George took a sip of tea, and as we ate, he asked us, "So, how go the dual investigations?"

"What are you talking about?" I asked as I nearly choked on a french fry.

"Come on. Your mother gets a threatening note, and then her doppelganger gets run over the very same day. I'd be disappointed in the two of you if you *weren't* digging into what happened to Betsy Wilkes."

"We might be," I said nonchalantly.

"Do you have any suspects yet?"

I was about to answer when Grace spoke before I could. "We'd be really interested in hearing who you have in mind."

"I've known Betsy Wilkes for more years than I care to remember, and I can't recall a single person who would want her dead, and that's a fact," George said.

"So, you think that hit-and-run was meant for my mother, too," I said.

The mayor lowered his voice. "It's entirely possible," he responded. "You can ask around town if you'd like, but I can't imagine anyone killing Betsy intentionally. But that's the key, isn't it? *Was* it intentional? People get distracted by many things these days, between chatting on their cell phones, listening to their radios, eating meals, and even putting on their makeup in the car. Sometimes I wonder that there aren't *more* accidents than there are, given the number of distractions we all face when we're driving around in our big metal machines."

"Do you honestly think it could have been an accident?" Grace asked him. "Myra Hickering said that it looked deliberate to her."

"Well, you have to take *anything* Myra tells you with a grain of salt," the mayor said.

"So it could have just been an accident after all," I said after finishing another bite.

"I didn't say that, either. It could have been, or it might just have been deliberate, but I doubt you'll find anything by digging into Betsy's life. That's all I'm saying. I'd love to hear what you've uncovered so far, if you have the time and interest to share with me."

I nodded. Sometimes it was easy to forget that once upon a time, long before he'd become our mayor, George Morris had been a cracker-jack police officer. Maybe it wouldn't be the worst thing in the world to share what we'd found with him so far.

But the diner was much too crowded to be the place for that particular conversation. "What are you doing after lunch, George?" I asked him as I polished off the rest of my fries.

"I was just going back to my office and ponder the future of our fair town in deep and mayoral thoughts," George said.

"In other words, you're going to take a nap on your couch," I replied softly.

"You know me too well, Suzanne. Why do you ask?"

"May we walk you back to City Hall?" I asked.

"Suzanne, the Jeep is parked at the donut shop, remember?" Grace asked.

"I know, but I could stretch my legs a little. How about you?" She got it instantly. "As a matter of fact, a stroll sounds perfect."

"What do you think, Mr. Mayor?" I asked him as I polished off the last bit of burger.

"I'll admit that it wouldn't hurt my reputation a bit to be seen walking around town with the two of you," he said with a grin.

I reached for his check so I could add it to ours, but he was too fast for me. "I appreciate the offer, but you know how I feel about accepting gratuities of any kind while I'm in office."

"Okay, but the day you leave office, I'm buying you breakfast, lunch, *and* dinner," I said with a smile.

"You're on," the mayor answered.

After we settled up with Trish, the three of us walked outside. The drizzle had let up, and the sun was even trying to peek out.

Once we were down the steps, George asked, "What's this really about? I know you two aren't doing it for the exercise, so why walk me back?"

"We thought we might take you up on your offer and get your opinion about where we were so far," I admitted.

"Away from a room full of eager listeners," George said, nodding his head in approval. "That's an excellent plan."

"We're glad you approve," Grace said. "That doesn't mean that we won't enjoy taking a stroll with you, too. You're not really that old, you know, and some women *like* men with more experience."

"Then maybe I'll find myself one of those," he said, "but in the meantime, tell me what you've discovered so far."

I was about to start when a familiar truck drove up and pulled into a spot a few feet from where we'd been walking.

Phillip Martin, former chief of police and current husband of my mother, got out and walked quickly toward us.

Chapter 16

"PHILLIP, WHAT ARE YOU doing back in town so soon? I thought you were on vacation," the mayor asked.

"I cut it short," he said. "Ladies, I'd appreciate a briefing on your status."

"We were just about to bring the mayor up to speed," I said. "Why don't you come up to his office? That way we only have to go over it all once."

"Sounds good to me," he said. "Lead on."

As we walked the rest of the way to City Hall, George asked Phillip, "How are you doing?"

"I'm nearly there," he said. "Maybe a little sore, and there are a few other issues we don't need to get into, but *any* day I'm vertical and not horizontal is a good day in my book. Why the interest in what's been happening with Dot?"

"She's not just a citizen in the town I represent," George said, "she's my friend, as well."

"Okay, I get that," Phillip answered.

We walked into the building and made our way upstairs to George's office. Once we took our seats inside, he closed the door.

"What happened to your latest secretary?" Grace asked him.

"It's a long story," the mayor replied, clearly not wanting to talk about it.

"We've got the time, if you'd care to share," I said, curious as to how he'd run yet another one off.

"Sorry, but I don't want to leave my wife alone any longer than I have to," Phillip interrupted. "Where do things stand?"

He had a right to hear what we'd uncovered so far. She may have been my mother, but she was his wife, and that entitled him to know what had been going on in his absence.

"We've ruled out Cordelia Bush and Francis Gray so far, at least on a provisional basis," I said.

"Why?" George asked.

"Cordelia has a busted leg, so we couldn't see her skulking around leaving Momma notes and then racing off before she could be caught. Francis claims that the note as it stands doesn't make sense as far as she's concerned, and we think she's right. After discussing both women with Momma further, she agrees with us."

"Okay, let's put a pin in both names for now," he allowed. "Who does that leave?"

"Gerard Mince is our number-one suspect at the moment," I said.

"He has reason to hate Dot, and his front fender is dented. By his own admission, it happened yesterday, which coincidentally is when Betsy Wilkes was run down," Grace added.

"What's Stephen Grant doing about it?" Phillip asked me.

"It's out of his jurisdiction, but we met the new chief of police for Maple Hollow, a tough woman named Liddy Holmes, and there's no doubt in our minds that she's going to dig into it."

"How did you happen to meet her?" George asked.

"Gerard called her to arrest us for trespassing in his garage," I admitted.

"There's a lot to unpack in that sentence," the mayor said. "I'm assuming you were there to see about the status of his fender. Why wasn't it breaking and entering, too?"

"Grace cracked the security code," I said proudly.

Both men looked at her with elevated levels of respect. Grace explained, "It wasn't that tough. The only two keys on the garage door bypass that had any smudges on them at all were the eight and the two. I got the combination on the second try, 8282."

"Still, it was clever of you to figure it out," Phillip said.

"It was Suzanne's idea to check the bypass," she said, defending my part in our plan.

"There's plenty of credit to go around," I replied. "The point is that when we pulled the tarp off of his car, we saw the dinged fender. Gerard pulled it down again though, and the police chief didn't get a chance to even look at it. When she started toward it, he told her that she needed a warrant to see it, and she backed off."

"Did you *ask* him what happened to his car?" the mayor asked us.

"We did. He claimed that he hit a tree in the fog last night coming back home," I explained.

"That could be true enough," George answered. "I was at a dinner in Maple Hollow last night, and I could barely see enough of the road to get home."

"Was it official business, or a date?" I asked him a bit mischievously.

"Doesn't matter," he answered gruffly, which meant that it had probably been a date.

"Any other suspects?" Phillip asked us.

"Yes, but you're not going to like it," I said.

"I can take it. I'm a big boy," he answered.

"Ellie Westmore," I said.

"Come on, Ellie might have had a little crush on me at one time, but I nipped it in the bud. Why do you think she might have had anything to do with the note Dorothea got?" he asked us.

"It was Momma's idea," I explained. "We were just following up on the leads she gave us herself. She seems to think this thing with Ellie is a little more serious than you suspect."

"Did anyone think to check her vehicle?" the mayor asked.

"We just got back from there," I admitted.

"Different make, different model, different color," Grace explained.

"And the fenders looked fine," I added.

"Okay, that just adds credence to the idea that she didn't do it," George said.

"Is anyone looking into Betsy's life?" Phillip asked. "The hit-and-run could have been intentional, but the killer might have gotten the right victim after all."

"You need to bear in mind that it could just as easily have been an accident," the mayor added.

"We are, but we need to do some more groundwork. George, Grace and I both trust your judgment about Betsy, but we need to dig into her life a little anyway. Do you mind?"

"Mind? Why should I mind? I said that I didn't think it was directed at her intentionally, but I could just as easily be wrong."

"Why exactly do we think Betsy Wilkes's death necessarily means that it was meant to be an attempt on my wife?" Phillip asked.

"They had the same build, the same hairdo, and they were even wearing identical jackets," Grace explained. "Plus, according to Myra Hickering, Betsy's back was turned to the road when she was struck and killed."

"So it might be a case of mistaken identity," Phillip observed.

"We think so, but that doesn't mean that Betsy might not have an enemy or two herself. It amazed me how many Momma could name right off the bat."

"It shouldn't," Phillip said. "Suzanne, your mother is an influential person in this area. She has a great many friends, but nearly as many enemies. In fact, I should be with her, just in case whoever might have tried to kill her goes for another try."

"She's not going to stand still for you hovering over her shoulder while she tries to conduct business, Phillip. You know that, don't you?"

"Of course I do," he answered with a snort. "That doesn't mean I'm going to let her dissuade me from doing it, though. Until you two are able to figure out what really happened, I'm going to shadow her every second she's away from the house."

"I don't envy you that," I told him sympathetically.

"No, but it's the *only* way I'll be able to live with myself," he acknowledged. As he stood, he added, "Keep me posted." He then shook hands with George. "I assume you're in on this, too?"

"I'll do as much as these ladies allow me to, but don't make the mistake of thinking that I'm in charge. This is Suzanne's case, and to a lesser extent, Grace's. I'm just the third team."

"Grace and I are equal partners in every case we investigate," I corrected him, "so that makes you the second team, not the third. Look at that. You've already gotten a promotion from where you thought you were."

After Phillip was gone, George asked, "Is there anything I can do?"

"You can put a little pressure on your connections in Maple Hollow to look into Gerard Mince's story and see if he *really* got that damaged fender hitting a tree, or something maybe a little more human than that."

"I can do that. I'll keep you posted on the results. Anything else?" he asked.

"Just keep your ears and eyes open," I said. "George, nothing can happen to my mother, especially not on my watch."

"I understand," he said gravely. "Happy hunting to the both of you."

"Thanks," we said simultaneously, and then we grinned at each other.

"I'm glad I'm not the culprit you two are chasing. Whoever it is, they don't stand a chance."

"That's what we're hoping," I said, and then Grace and I left the mayor's office and headed back to Donut Hearts, where I'd left my Jeep.

There was a piece of folded paper under the windshield wiper when we got back.

"Butt out, or you two could be next."

"Well, will you look at that?" I asked as I handed the note gingerly to Grace. "It appears that we've made ourselves noticeable."

"If it's from the stalker/killer and not the mad note leaver," she said as she frowned at the message.

"I'm thinking this is more along the lines of the note Momma got," I said. "Look at the font and the paper they used. It's a match to the one left at her cottage, not the other notes that showed up all over town. We've at least attracted the bad guy's attention."

"And that's a good thing why exactly?" Grace asked me with a grin.

"It means that we're getting closer than we thought we were," I told her.

"I'm glad at least *someone* thinks so," Grace answered. "Suzanne, do you honestly think we're going to find something in Betsy's life that someone would kill her over?"

"I don't, but that doesn't mean that we don't check anyway," I told her. "Besides, I'm not sure what else we can do. I'm counting on Chief Holmes to dig into Gerard's story, and the mayor to push her to do it quickly. That's really all we can do about Gerard, and we need something more if we're going to speak with Ellie Westmore again. All that really leaves us is looking into Betsy's life. Who knows? Maybe we will find a lead to her real killer, but if not, at least we might be able to eliminate the theory that she was the intended victim all along. If that's the case, perhaps the note Momma got was just a random piece of spite after all."

"Is it wrong of me to hope that's what it really was?" Grace asked.

"No, but it doesn't seem likely, not after we get a new note like this one," I said, folding it back up and putting it in the Jeep.

"Should we tell anyone we got it?" Grace asked me as I started the vehicle and started off to speak with Betsy's neighbors and friends.

"Maybe we keep it under wraps, at least for now," I said as I drove. "If we tell Stephen, George, or even Phillip, we're going to get so much protection that we aren't going to be able to do our job, which is to find out what really happened to Betsy and who has it in for my mother." I glanced over at Grace and saw that she was biting her nail. "Is that okay with you?"

"It's fine," she said. "I'm not really eager to speak with Stephen before I'm ready, and if we tell George or Phillip, the first call that either of them makes after calling the other one is to my boyfriend."

"The man who would be your fiancé," I corrected.

She ignored my comment. "Let's just dig a little more and see where we are in a few hours."

"Agreed," I said. Really, what else could we do, given the circumstances?

At least that's what I thought at the time.

Chapter 17

"SO, YOU'VE NEVER HEARD of anyone having a problem with Betsy?" we asked her third neighbor after interviewing all of her friends we could find. So far, no one had the slightest quarrel with the woman. I was beginning to think that we'd *never* find one single person willing to say one word against her. Part of it could have been the fact that a great many people wouldn't speak ill of the dead, but most of it was probably because Betsy had been a genuinely nice, if somewhat quirky, person.

"Well, I wouldn't say never," the older man said. "Hang on one second." He vanished for a minute, and when he returned, he was wiping his hands on a dish towel. "I've been trying to get Old Sal to eat, but I'm not having much luck. I'm about to feed him my steak if I have to. He knows something happened to Betsy, there's no doubt in my mind."

"You took him in?" I asked, my admiration for the man soaring.

"Well, we're a pair of old widower bachelors, so once we get used to each other, we'll be fine."

"About Betsy," Grace reminded him.

"Oh yes. I know for a fact that she had words with Myra Hickering once."

"What?" I asked, startled by the confession. "Did you say Myra?"

"I did indeed," he answered, a bit confused by my reaction.

"What did it involve, Mr. Nichols?" Grace asked. "Can you remember?"

"And when exactly did it happen?" I asked in follow-up.

"It must have been six months ago," the older man said after giving it a moment's thought. "Maybe seven, but not more than eight."

"It was this year, though," I asserted.

"Oh, definitely. I'm sure of at least that much." He looked pleased to be so certain about the timing of it.

"What was the argument about?"

"I couldn't say," Mr. Nichols said, "but I'm sure there was something volatile about it. After all, they were facing off in Myra's yard at the time. It looked quite heated to me. I'm sorry, but that's all I know."

"Thanks," I said.

"Are you certain you wouldn't like to come in? I could make us some nice tea, and we could chat further. I'm sure Old Sal would love the company."

We'd already refused his offer three times. "We appreciate it, but we really must be going," Grace said sweetly.

"If you must, then," he said sadly, but then he brightened for a moment. "Feel free to come back anytime. We don't have to talk about Betsy or Myra, or even Old Sal. I have the most fascinating collection of nineteenth-century European stamps that are quite absorbing!"

"We'll bear it in mind," I said.

"What do you make of that?" I asked Grace as we got back into the Jeep.

"He's just a lonely old man. I'm glad Old Sal found a new home with him."

"I don't mean the dog, and I'm not going to look at his stamp collection, I don't care how lonely he is," I said smartly. "I'm talking about what he said about Myra and Betsy."

"Suzanne, what does it matter? If we can be sure that one person in town was *not* driving that car, it has to be Myra Hickering. She was the first one on the scene, remember?"

"Maybe so, maybe not. It was all a bit of chaos though, wasn't it? What if Myra was racing home and she didn't see Betsy until it was too late? She had time to hit her with her car, race around back to her carport, and then rush out front before anyone else got there." The more I considered the scenario, the more a possibility it became in my mind. What better way to disguise your involvement than to be the first responder at the scene of the accident?

"I suppose it's possible," Grace allowed.

I started driving toward Myra's place, a short jaunt from where we'd interviewed Mr. Nichols.

"What are we going to say to her?" Grace asked me.

"I'd like to ask her about the argument, but what I really want to do is see her car," I answered.

Myra opened the door and smiled at us before we could even ring the bell. "What can I do for you ladies?"

"Why did you have an argument on your front lawn with Betsy Wilkes six or seven months ago?" I asked her, jumping straight to the nitty gritty.

Myra's smile vanished quickly, and I saw her entire body tense up. "I'm sure I don't know what you're talking about."

"Really? Should we bring our eyewitness over here and have them recount the story to you?" Grace asked. "Myra, what happened?"

"It was that cat of hers," Myra said with anger. "It refused to stay at Betsy's and would haunt my birdfeeders and bird baths, stalking my little friends as though they were prey. Why is it that dogs have to be leashed and collared and live their lives behind electrified fences but cats are free to roam wherever they please?" It was clear this was a real sore point with Myra.

"So, you confronted her about it," I said calmly. "You sound as though you were furious about the situation."

"We had a few words," Myra admitted, "but soon after that, someone hit her cat with their car, and the problems suddenly stopped."

Had the hit-and-run driver taken out the cat first, and then later, its owner? That was holding a grudge a little too long and hard, at least as far as I was concerned. "Did they ever find out who hit her cat?" Grace asked, her thoughts clearly paralleling mine.

"They discovered that some teenaged boy was driving his truck too fast after school," Myra said, and then she looked sharply at each of us in turn. "*I* certainly didn't do it, and I'm appalled you could even think that I would. I treasure *all* life, whether it be avian, feline, or human."

"Would you mind if we looked at your vehicle while we're here?" I asked her as innocently as I could manage. "We just want to be able to eliminate you as a suspect entirely."

Myra frowned for so long that I was certain she was going to throw us off her property, but she finally just shrugged. "If I don't, the news will be spread all over town that I ran poor Betsy down myself within the hour, so I might as well cooperate with you and be done with it."

"Hang on a second," I said as Myra took a step off the porch. "Grace and I don't spread rumors. If we have a problem with someone, or a question, we go talk to them, face to face, like we're doing right now with you." There was no humor, no levity in my voice. Starting rumors was serious business, and Grace and I might be many things, but we weren't gossips. "You owe us both an apology, Myra," I said.

I honestly wasn't expecting to get one, but Myra surprised me by looking instantly remorseful. "Of course. You're right. I'm sorry. It was just all so traumatic! You can't imagine the scars it's left on my heart, and the nightmares I had last night. I keep thinking if I'd just been a little more observant, I could have warned her somehow, but I just stood there at my window and watched it all unfold like some kind of bad movie."

"It's okay, Myra," I said, and Grace nodded as well.

My partner added, "You don't have to show us anything."

I begged to differ, and if Myra agreed, I was going to have to push her on it, despite what Grace had just told her. I *needed* to see her car before I could move on, and one way or the other, I was going to see it.

Myra shook her head, though. "No, I'm happy to show you." She led us down her walk and around the house to her carport. It surprised me how many homes in the area didn't have full garages. Even though we were still in the south, we got a few snows a year, and the cold visited us for several months, but the builders, especially in the seventies and eighties, hadn't seemed to take that into account by providing full walls and a functioning door.

I was surprised to see *two* cars parked there, not just one. "I didn't even realize that you had a Cadillac," I said as I touched the dusty hood of one of her vehicles. I didn't need to walk around it, or the small SUV parked beside it, to see that neither vehicle had been involved in a collision anytime lately, certainly not the afternoon before.

"It was my late husband's," Myra admitted.

"But John's been dead for five years," I said.

"I know, but I can't bear the thought of getting rid of it. I let the plates expire, but it gives me comfort seeing it parked there beside my car. It's as though he never left, you know? Besides, it's such a bother getting rid of it, even if it weren't a sentimental attachment. I just never seemed to have the steam to do it, if you know what I mean."

I understood. As angry as I'd been with Max after the divorce, there had been a few mementos of his I'd hung onto. To this day I couldn't explain why, but it didn't really matter. "Sorry to bother you, Myra. I hope you know that we weren't accusing you of anything."

"We just have to follow up *all* of the leads we get," Grace added sympathetically.

"I just hope you find whoever killed poor Betsy. We might have had our differences, but no one deserved to be struck down like that."

"I'm sorry you had to witness it," I said as I touched her shoulder lightly.

"Thank you for that, Suzanne."

Once we were back in the Jeep and on our way, Grace said, "We should get Mr. Nichols and Myra together."

I had to laugh at the thought of the unlikely pairing. "Why on earth would we ever do that?" I asked her as I pulled out onto Springs Drive.

"They're both lonely. Why can't they be lonely together?" she asked.

"For a woman sitting on a proposal, you seem awfully romantic when it comes to other people's lives," I said. "I know I'm not supposed to ask, but I can't help myself. Have you made up your mind about Stephen's proposal yet?"

"I'm going to say yes," she said as though she'd announced that she was on her way to the gas station.

"Wow, you sound so happy about it," I remarked dryly.

"Oh, I am. It's just that I don't relish giving up my independence. I've always been a bit of a loner, and I'm not sure how having a husband underfoot is going to suit me, but I love him, and my life is better with him than without him, so I suppose I might as well marry him and get it over with."

I pulled the Jeep over onto a wide part of the shoulder and stopped the vehicle. "Grace, nobody is saying you have to marry him, but if you do, you two can decide what your lives together are going to look like. Every marriage is different. Besides, can you really see Stephen Grant as the type of man being underfoot all of the time, as you so eloquently put it?"

She stopped frowning and smiled for a moment. "No, I don't suppose I do."

"Take my advice," I said. "Don't say anything to him until you're sure it's what you want. Do that for me, would you?"

"Suzanne, I'm not at all certain that I'll ever be one hundred percent sure of anything," she admitted.

"Then there's your answer," I told her. "If it isn't right for you, it isn't right, and no amount of hoping or wishing is going to make it otherwise."

Grace frowned at me. "Let me get this straight. The woman who's been shoving me toward finding a husband is now telling me that I don't need one. Is that what you're saying?"

"No, not at all. I'm a big fan of having a husband, but I've had the bad kind, too, and I knew after being married to Max that I'd rather be alone than with someone who made me miserable. Jake just happens to make me happy, so I'm much better off with him than without him. It depends more on the fit than it does the man. I'm sure Max and Emily will be happy together. They're certainly a much better fit than we ever were."

"Speaking of your ex, I wonder if he ever showed up," Grace said.

"I've been wondering the same thing myself." I called his phone number, but I didn't get an answer, so I called Emily at her newsstand.

"Two Cows and a Moose," Emily answered brightly. "How may I help you?"

"Hey, Emily, it's Suzanne. Did Max ever turn up?"

"He did," she said happily. "It turns out that he had an audition in New York."

"And he didn't tell you about it?" I asked her worriedly. Was Max reverting to his old self once they'd said their vows?

"He did, or at least he tried to. I just never received the news. He sent me flowers with an explanation, but they never made it to my doorstep. When he finally got my voicemails, he called in a panic that I thought he'd abandoned me. We're good, Suzanne. I've got to say though that he was relieved that I told you, so he didn't have to."

"Well, I'm glad it all worked out," I said.

"It's going to be different for me from what you went through," Emily said softly. "*He's* different."

"I can see that, too. Maybe it's because this time he married the right woman," I replied with a smile.

"The truth is that he was dreadful to you, and he knows it. He told me that a day doesn't go by that he doesn't regret cheating on you, and everything that happened before that in your marriage. The reminder of what he's done in the past makes him try hard every day not to let it ever happen again. I'm sorry you had to go through it, but I'm glad you found Jake. You two are perfect for each other."

"I couldn't agree with you more," I said. "Well, I'll let you go. I know you must be busy."

"Not really," she said cheerfully.

"Okay then, I have to ask. What's the part he's up for?"

"He's auditioning for a commercial to play a young girl's exasperated father," she said with a giggle. "He's not happy about it. Max still sees himself as a twenty-something stallion, not a thirty-something papa."

I had to laugh along with her. "At least he's still getting auditions."

"That's what he says," she said, and then I heard a voice say from the other end, "Do you have the latest *Movieland Horror* in yet?"

"Hang on, Timmy, I'll be right with you." Then she got back to me. "Gotta run, Suzanne. Thanks again for caring."

"You bet," I said.

After I hung up, I said, "The Case of the Missing Ex has been solved. Max is on a commercial audition, and they got their signals crossed."

"Well, at least that's a relief," Grace said. "Where are we now in our investigation?"

"I'm not sure," I said. "Something is nagging at the back of my mind, but I can't put my finger on it. I feel as though we've seen something significant, but I don't know what it might be."

"It's happened to you before, Suzanne," she said. "Try not to think about it, and maybe it will come to you."

"Okay, I'll do my best not to think about pink elephants. Whoops, there goes another one," I answered with a grin. "But if I'm doing everything in my power *not* to think about the clue or hint or whatever it is I'm missing, then what should I do?"

"That's a fair question," Grace said.

"Okay, but what I need to know is this: what is a good answer?"

She was saved from responding when my cell phone rang.

Chapter 18

"HELLO, MR. MAYOR. Don't tell me you have news for us already," I said after putting my phone on its speaker setting so Grace could hear, too.

"It's amazing how people respond to the gravity of my office," he said, and I could hear a hint of a smile in his voice. "As a matter of fact, I just spoke with Chief Holmes."

"What did she have to say?" Grace asked. "Hey, George. It's me."

"Hi, me," he answered. "Holmes got the warrant, and she has a friend with the state police who was already in town on another matter who's some kind of expert on vehicular homicides."

"Is he working a case of it in Maple Hollow, too?" I asked. That was just too big a coincidence for me to take. Maybe we had a serial hit-and-run driver, and what happened to Betsy Wilkes wasn't just an isolated incident.

"No, he's divorced, and he was dropping his daughter off," the mayor said.

I took a stab in the dark. "Was he once married to the police chief, by any chance?" I asked.

"Suzanne, you may have missed your calling. That's a pretty astute deduction. Yes, apparently the divorce was amicable, and the chief decided to call in a favor from her ex-husband. Some divorced spouses get along better apart than they ever did when they were together."

"I know Max and I do," I said. "He's been found, by the way, not that he was ever really lost. Have you heard?"

"No," the mayor said. "Where was he hiding?"

"He had a commercial audition in New York, and Emily never got the message," I said. "What did the chief have to say?"

"It is in her ex's expert opinion that Gerard Mince did indeed hit a tree last night. Sorry, I know you were hoping for better news."

A thought crossed my mind just as Grace expressed it. "Just because he hit a tree doesn't necessarily mean that he didn't hit Betsy, too."

"True," George Morris said.

"Is there any way to find that out?" I asked.

"I can always check with the police chief," the mayor said. "Still, I'd keep digging if I were you. In the meantime, is there anything else I can do?"

"No, there's nothing else I can think of," I admitted. "The truth is, Grace and I are kind of stymied about what our next move should be, too."

"Would you like some friendly advice from a former cop worth exactly what you have to pay for it?" George asked.

"You bet we would," I said. "And don't sell yourself short, Mr. Mayor. You were a very good cop once upon a time."

"I appreciate that," he said. "Sometimes folks around here seem to forget that I was ever on the force at all."

"That's because you're so good at the job you've got now," Grace said with a smile.

He must have heard it in her voice, though he couldn't see us. "Flattery will get you everywhere, young lady."

"The advice?" I reminded him.

"Go back over the basics of what you know, what you think, and what you suspect," he said. "Do it on paper if you need to, but it never hurts to refresh things when you're stuck. At least it's worked for me in the past."

"We'll do that," I said. "Thanks for the tip."

"All part of the service," he said, and then he hung up.

I was about to say something when I saw flashing lights in my rearview mirror. We weren't even driving! What possible offense could we have committed being pulled safely off to the side of the road while we'd talked?

And then I saw the police chief get out of his cruiser and approach us.

At least he didn't have his weapon drawn.

To no one's surprise, he went to the passenger door, not mine. Tapping on the glass with his flashlight, he told Grace, "I need to talk to you."

"If it's about the report on Gerard Mince's car, we just got it," Grace told him after she rolled down her window.

"This isn't business. It's personal," he said.

Grace looked over at me before she opened her door.

"Go," I told her.

"What do I tell him?" she whispered.

"I've found that the truth is usually the best place to start," I said.

"Okay," she answered as she got out and faced him.

At least she'd left her window down. I wasn't even going to pretend that I wasn't eavesdropping, and what was more, I was certain that Grace knew it, too.

"This is driving me crazy," Stephen Grant told her after a moment. "I need to know what you're thinking. Do you love me or not?" He blurted out the question as though it was something that had to come out, and he had no choice in the matter.

"I do," she said simply.

"Then why don't you say yes?" There was a real tone of hurt in his voice.

"Because it's not that simple," she answered.

"It can be," he said.

"Stephen, I've been on my own for fifteen years. Ever since my folks died, it's just been me."

"That's not entirely true. You've had Suzanne, her mother, shoot, the entire town of April Springs," he protested. "Not to mention for the last couple of years, I've been in your life."

"In it, but not all of it," Grace said seriously.

To my surprise, and I'm sure my best friend's as well, he began to laugh.

"What's so funny?"

"Grace, I don't expect you to quit your job and stay home, cook and clean for me, and grant my every wish."

"That's a good thing then, because you would be sincerely disappointed if those were your expectations," she answered frostily.

He didn't back down though, not a single step, which was another point in his favor, at least as far as I was concerned. Then again, my point of view didn't matter. Grace's was the only one that counted at the moment.

"Why do things have to be all that much different than they are now? I'd like to think that our lives will be enhanced by being around each other more, not diminished. I don't expect to be on a tight leash once we're married, and I don't expect you to be, either. We both have pretty demanding careers, and lives too for that matter, but wouldn't it be nice to share our downtime with each other? I can't speak for you, but when I'm around you, the good things are twice as nice, and the bad ones are half as rotten. I love you, and I want to be with you. I don't want to change you, and I don't expect you to try to change me. At least as far as I'm concerned, the fact that we love each other and want to be together is really all that matters. Everything else is just details and logistics."

Good for him! I'd never heard him make that kind of speech in his life. In fact, I wasn't sure I'd ever heard *any* man express his feelings so eloquently. Jake was awesome, but he wasn't much of a talker when it came to his emotions.

"Do you really think it's that simple?" Grace asked him.

"If we don't overthink it, it can be," he replied.

In a voice that was almost too softly spoken for me to hear, she said, "Okay, then."

"I'm sorry, what was that?" he asked her.

"You heard me," she replied a little stronger.

"I didn't. I honestly didn't."

"I said okay then," she repeated with a great deal more force.

"Okay then what?" he asked, clearly confused by her response.

"Yes. I'll marry you," she said, and this time everybody in our part of April Springs must have heard it, she said it so loudly.

Chapter 19

WHEN SHE GOT BACK INTO the car after a lengthy kiss, Grace turned and grinned at me as she showed me the ring Stephen had just placed on her finger. "So, that just happened."

"And how do we feel about it?" I asked her.

"We're ecstatic," she answered with a laugh. "How could I say no to that?"

"I was about to marry him if you didn't, and I've already got a husband," I said as I joined her in her laughter. "I'm so happy for you."

"So am I," Grace said, but then the grin died a little. "That doesn't mean that we still don't have something we need to do. Is it time to make up the list that George suggested?"

"There's no need to write anything down," I said as I started the Jeep and headed back to Ellie Westmore's house. "There's something back at her house that I want to check, and then I want to speak with her one more time."

"Do you see any sign of her?" I asked Grace as I parked well away from the house in question. It had been a mistake parking so close to Gerard Mince's garage when we'd been there before, and I wasn't going to make the same one again.

"It appears that she's still gone," Grace said.

"Maybe so, but I want to ring the doorbell first anyway. There is no way I want to get caught snooping twice in one day."

We rang the bell for two solid minutes without any response.

"The coast must be clear," Grace said. "What exactly is it that we're looking for?"

"Come on around back, and I'll tell you," I told her as I made my way to Ellie Westmore's carport.

"That's what I thought," I said as I knelt down and touched my finger to an oil stain I'd seen earlier on the carport's concrete floor. "This is fresh. It had to have been where I'd picked up the oil on my shoe. I saw it before, but I didn't put two and two together."

"I see it now, but I'm not sure that means anything," Grace said. "So her car's leaking oil. It happens."

"That's the thing. Her car hasn't been parked here," I explained as I got down on my hands and knees. Taking out my cell phone, I turned on the flashlight app and shone it onto the concrete beneath her car.

It was clean.

"Another car's been parked here until recently," I said as I switched off my light and used the phone for its original intended purpose, to make a call. I started to lean against the wall, but the tools hanging there made it impossible.

"Who are you calling?"

"Stephen," I said.

The line was busy, though.

"Okay, let me try George," I said as I placed the next call.

He picked up right away.

"George, it's Suzanne. I need to know the make and model of the vehicle that Ellie Westmore's husband, Homer, used to drive."

"I'm on it. Let me get right back to you," he said.

After I hung up, Grace nodded. "I think I understand. Seeing Myra's late husband's car told you that it might not be that unusual for a widow to hold onto her husband's vehicle, so that made you wonder about what Homer used to drive."

"That, and the fresh oil stain on my tennis shoes," I admitted. "It was worth checking, and this time, it paid off. I've got a hunch that we're about to learn that Homer Westmore's car was used to run down Betsy Wilkes, and unless I miss my guess, Ellie is the one who threatened Momma and then us, too."

"Very good, Suzanne," a voice said as someone stepped out from the bushes that shielded the carport in back.

It was Ellie Westmore, and evidently she'd just watched as we'd figured out that she was the killer after all.

Chapter 19

"COME ON, MRS. WESTMORE. You're not really going to shoot a former student, are you?" I asked her as I saw the handgun she trained on us.

"I didn't even know Homer *owned* a gun until he was already dead and I was going through his things," she said as she waved the gun around in the air. "He knew that I detested the things, but that didn't seem to matter to him. Honestly, if I'd known about this, he might have died in a very different way than me dosing his food with quite a bit too much of his heart medication."

"Are you admitting that you killed your husband, too?" Grace asked her.

"I didn't *make* him eat that doctored lasagna; I just didn't stop him," she said, and then with a hint of bizarre laughter, she added, "After all, it's not like I held a gun to his head," she said as she waved it around in the air.

Had my former teacher snapped completely? I knew that George would be calling me back soon, so maybe I could answer it without Ellie Westmore noticing. If the mayor knew what was going on, he could send help.

I knew that it wasn't much, but at the moment, it was the best plan that I had.

"The police and the mayor know that it was you driving Homer's car," I said, trying to reason with her. "There's no reason to kill us."

"Didn't I tell you? I reported the car stolen right after I ran Betsy Wilkes over. I can't tell you what a shock it was when I saw her face at the last second. I could have sworn it was your mother, Suzanne! Everything matched: her build, her hairstyle, even her coat! How was I supposed to know?"

"Well, for starters, you didn't have to go after my mother in the first place," I said, trying to keep my voice calmer than I felt.

"She stole Phillip from me," Ellie Westmore said gruffly. "I had no choice."

"How is that even possible?" Grace asked her. "You were still married to Homer when Dot and Phillip started dating! She didn't take anything from you, because Chief Martin was never yours to begin with!"

"He should have been; that's the entire point," my former teacher explained, using a tone of voice I was well familiar with. "I just took too long getting rid of Homer. I thought I could accept the fact that Phillip was with Dot, but after my husband's death, he was there for me. The man was so sweet, so sympathetic, that I knew that we had to be together, no matter what."

"But he told you that he loved my mother," I said, wondering where the mayor was and what was taking him so long to call me back. How long could we stall this crazy woman? She'd proven that she could kill twice so far, and I had a feeling that doubling her score wasn't going to faze her in the least.

"So, what's the plan now? You have to get rid of Grace and me, then you have to kill Momma. Do you honestly think Phillip is going to rush into your arms with his entire family dead? It doesn't even matter if he doesn't realize that you were responsible for killing the people he loved, he's not going to want to have anything to do with you!" I knew that I should have been calmer, and that I should have been trying to get her to see logic and reason, but I just couldn't bring myself to do it. She had to know that even if she managed to kill all three of us, Phillip would never be hers.

If that ultimate goal was taken away from her, then there'd be no reason to kill us.

That wasn't strictly true, though.

Grace and I now knew what she'd done.

In essence, she had no choice but to get rid of us.

That meant that it was up to us to somehow turn the tables on her before she had a chance to shoot us in cold blood.

Grace must have realized that I'd been quiet for too long, so she stepped in. "Why leave the note in the first place?" she asked her. "Wouldn't it have been smarter just to go after Dot without giving her fair warning first?"

"Yes, I thought about that after the fact," Ellie Westmore admitted. "It was just that when I heard about those notes being left all over town, I figured it would be a wonderful time to tweak Dot a little."

"So, you didn't know anything in particular that she got away with," I said.

"Your mother has been skirting business ethics and the law for too long *not* to have done something in the past that wouldn't stand up under scrutiny," she said churlishly. "I decided to allow her imagination to supply the specifics. Then I realized that it wouldn't be enough, so I knew that I had to take more direct action."

"That's when you ran down a perfectly innocent woman," I said. Where was that blasted mayor, anyway, and why wasn't he calling back? My plan hinged on him being prompt, and it looked like I'd misjudged the situation.

"Oh, Betsy wasn't innocent," the killer said. "I'm sure there were at least a few sins in her past she needed to pay for."

It was hard to believe that a woman I'd once idolized had gone so utterly and completely around the bend. Well, if George wasn't going to be able to save us, I needed to do something myself. There were gardening tools just behind me, but if I made a move for one of them, there was a good chance Ellie Westmore would shoot at least one of us. I glanced over at Grace, and then at the tools, and she seemed to get the idea instantly.

Now all that we needed was a distraction.

George Morris might not be there in person, but he was about to give us a hand in spirit, whether he realized it or not.

"George, thank goodness you're here! Look out, she's got a gun!" I said with as much emotion in my voice as I could muster. "She's lost her mind. Stop her!"

As Ellie whirled around to face someone who wasn't there, Grace and I both jumped toward the hanging tools.

I grabbed the clippers while she went after the scythe.

Without hesitation, we charged Ellie Westmore with the only weapons we had close at hand.

We both must have known instinctively that if we tried to run away, she'd shoot us in the back.

There was no flight available to us, only fight.

Chapter 20

ELLIE WAS TOO QUICK for us, though. The instant she saw that George was nowhere in sight, she spun back around toward us.

Grace was moving in with her weapon, but it was going to be too late for me.

Ellie Westmore pointed the gun at my heart, and I dropped the shears in my hand as she pulled the trigger.

Chapter 21

ONLY NOTHING HAPPENED!

Either it was unloaded or the safety was still on, but the only thing that mattered was that I was still alive!

Grace tried to knock the gun out of her hand with her long-handled tool, but she missed! It wasn't her fault. Ellie pulled her hand away at the last second, and Grace lost her balance, tripping on a lawn trimmer that was sticking out from the wall.

She was on the floor in front of the killer, powerless.

I might not have had a weapon in my hand anymore, but *I* wasn't helpless.

Throwing myself at Ellie Westmore, I hit my former third grade teacher with all of my might in the face.

What would have gotten me rightfully thrown out of school so many years before might have just saved our lives.

Grace leaned over the unconscious killer as I retrieved the gun. It was loaded all right, but Homer must have had the safety on. Ellie Westmore's ignorance about guns may have just saved me.

"She's out cold, Suzanne. Wow, that was some punch."

"I did what I had to do," I said. After I pocketed the gun, I got some rope from the wall and tied her hands and feet thoroughly. "Let her get out of that."

I was about to call Chief Grant when my cell phone rang.

It was the mayor, finally.

"Sorry about that. I got held up, but I've got the information for you. Homer Westmore drove a dark-blue SUV, and you're not going to believe what else I found out."

"It was reported stolen right after the hit-and-run," I said as I tried to catch my breath. I was usually fine in the heat of the moment, but after confronting a killer, all I wanted to do was crawl into a corner and cry.

At least I had things in the right order.

The mayor sounded disappointed. "How did you know?"

"Ellie Westmore just confessed to killing not only Betsy Wilkes, but her late husband, too," I said calmly.

"Where are you, Suzanne?"

"We're back in Ellie's carport. Don't worry. She tried to kill us, but Grace and I stopped her. Do you think you might be able to call the police chief for us? I hit Ellie in the face and knocked her out, but I'm not sure how long she's going to stay out."

"This is real," George said in a statement more than a question.

"As real as it gets," he said.

"I'm on it."

In less than four minutes, we heard the first sirens.

Ellie Westmore finally began to stir, which was a relief to me. I had wanted to incapacitate her, not kill her. "You struck me! You actually struck me! How dare you, Suzanne Hart!"

"It's a little late for righteous indignation, Ellie," I said, "and I don't think you can send me to the principal's office, either."

"Untie me this instant," she snapped. "I demand it!"

"I don't think so," Grace answered. "We're back here," she shouted out as the sirens died and we heard running footsteps.

The chief was leading the pack, but instead of worrying about the killer lying subdued on the ground, he went straight to his fiancée. "There's no chance you're going to give up solving cases with Suzanne once we get married, is there?"

She grinned as she embraced him. "What do you think?"

As he pulled away, he said, "Hey, you can't blame a guy for asking."

"You've asked all of the questions you get to for the moment. I said yes, remember?" Grace asked as two officers helped Ellie Westmore up.

I noticed the bemused look on one of the officers' faces as he said, "And you said that I'd never amount to anything."

She didn't even reply as he untied her feet. I did notice that he waited until she was cuffed before he pulled all of the rope off of her hands.

As they led her away, she looked back at us and frowned. "You always were a disappointment, Suzy."

"Right back at you, Teach," I said with a grin. "I don't know about you, but I'll find a way to live with it on my end."

George showed up as they were loading Ellie into the back of the squad car. "Good work, ladies," he said. "As always, you were one step ahead of everyone else."

"What can I say?" I told him. "We got the right puzzle pieces first. Wow, if I hadn't heard her confession with my own ears, I never would have believed it. Do you think there's a chance a jury will convict her?"

"If any of her former students are empaneled, I have a hunch they might," he said with a wicked grin.

"You reap what you sow," I said. "I need to call Momma and tell her that it's all over."

"I already took care of that. She and Phillip are on their way," George said as I shook my open hand around a bit. "Is there something wrong?"

"I think I might have broken my hand when I hit Ellie Westmore in the face, but even if I did, it was totally worth it."

Chapter 22

THE NEXT NIGHT AT DINNER, I pretended to study my stepfather for a few moments before speaking. "I look and look and look, but I still don't get it."

"Get what?" he asked as he took another serving of meatloaf. He'd certainly gotten his appetite back after the surgery and the ensuing recovery time.

"I mean, I suppose *some* women might find you attractive, but handsome enough to kill for? I just don't see it."

"He has many more charms than just his looks," Momma said as she squeezed her husband's hand.

"Ladies, could we please not talk about me this way? I feel responsible enough as it is for what happened."

"Phillip, I keep telling you that *none* of this is your fault. The woman fixated on you, but you never encouraged her with anything more than kindness."

"Momma's right," I told him. "You should listen to her."

"I'm sorry, what did you just say?" my mother asked me with a grin.

"I'm not repeating it," I said as my phone rang. "It's Jake!" I said. "Do you mind if I take it?"

"By all means," Momma said.

I stepped out onto the porch as I answered the call. "Where are you? Are you going to be back soon?" He had told me earlier when I'd caught him up on what had been happening in April Springs that he'd solved the case and was on his way back after wrapping up a few loose ends.

"I just left the cottage, but you weren't there," he said.

"I'm at Momma's. Come on over. We had meatloaf, but there are plenty of leftovers."

"That sounds amazing. Are you sure she won't mind?"

"Positive," I said. "You sound awfully pleased with yourself." It was good to hear my husband happy again, and if it meant that he had to spend half his days away from me to be that way, then that was going to be fine with me.

"I am," he said. "You know the department didn't have a big budget to spend on my services, right?"

"I'm well aware of it," I said. "You didn't exactly do this for the money. You needed to get back on your feet again."

"I'm glad you feel that way, because I didn't get any."

"Any what? They didn't pay you *anything*?" I asked him. We were doing okay, but the truth was I wouldn't have minded a bit more in our weekly budget.

"I didn't say that," he said with a grin, and then I heard an old-fashioned horn blow. When I looked toward it, I saw Jake driving a baby-blue truck that had to be sixty years old if it was a day, though the gleaming new paint job didn't give it away.

As he parked it in front of me and got out, he asked, "Isn't she beautiful? She's a 1959 Ford pickup with a narrow bed. The engine's been rebuilt, and it runs like a top. The chief loves to find old vehicles and restore them as a hobby, so we decided to barter for my services."

"Wow. What kind of gas mileage does it get?"

"Well, there's a lot of steel here," he said as he patted the fender. "You know that I've always wanted one."

"Then I'm glad you got it," I said. "Did you trade your truck for it, too?"

"No, a couple of guys from the force are bringing it back this weekend for me," he said. "This is just for fun."

"Then I'm glad you're enjoying it," I said.

"Want to take a ride in it?"

"Don't you want to eat first?" I asked.

"I guess," he answered, his tone the same as a little boy who just learned that he couldn't play with his friends until he ate his broccoli.

"You know what? Let me just tell Momma and Phillip what we're doing, and we'll take it for a spin around the block."

The joy on his face was everything to me, and as I ducked inside to tell them the news, I was so happy that I had Jake in my life.

The extra money might have been nice, but the look on his face was worth more than a million dollars to me.

RECIPES

Harvest-Fresh Baked Apples

In my house, nothing says autumn like baked apples, and we love making these the afternoon we get back from picking our own apples at the orchard. This recipe has the added bonus of making the house smell like the holidays, and the taste of these is amazing as well. As hard as it is to resist the temptation, we like to wait until these cool off some after they come out of the oven, but we never wait long enough, because they are so tempting. There are times we enjoy these plain—as if this recipe could ever be called plain!—and times we like to add some vanilla bean ice cream or even heavy whipping cream. No matter how you serve them, though, give these a try, because they are truly delightful!

Ingredients

3 medium- to large-sized apples (Granny Smith work, but so does any firm and crisp apple)

½ cup brown sugar, light

½ teaspoon cinnamon

½ teaspoon nutmeg

pinch salt

3 tablespoons butter, divided into thirds

1 tablespoon vanilla extract, divided into thirds

Optional

½ teaspoon allspice

1½ cups apple cider or apple juice (water is acceptable, too)

Directions

Preheat oven to 360 degrees. In a medium-sized mixing bowl, combine ½ cup brown sugar, ½ teaspoon cinnamon, ½ teaspoon nutmeg, and a pinch of salt. Now is the time to add the allspice if you are so inclined.

Wash each apple and then core out the center, leaving ¼ to ½ inch at the bottom. Pack the cavity with equal amounts of the mix and then top with 1 teaspoon of vanilla extract to each apple. Finally, add a tablespoon pat of butter to each apple.

Place in an oven-safe dish and leave enough room to add 1½ cups of apple juice or cider to the bottom of the dish.

Bake the apples for 45 minutes, removing them from the oven at the halfway point and basting the apple interiors with liquid from the bottom.

Let cool to warm, and then enjoy by themselves, or with ice cream or heavy cream if desired.

Makes three servings

Cranberry Dark Chocolate Donuts

T here are times when I want a quick treat, and other times when I like to laze around in my kitchen coming up with new and exotic recipes to share with all of you. This one definitely goes under the first category.

I like keeping a supply of staples in my pantry, especially as cold weather approaches. We get a handful of snowfalls in my part of North Carolina, but it's much likelier to be cold and rainy instead. Those are days I like to stay in, read, binge on my favorite shows, and bake, so anything I've got on hand is fair game.

This recipe uses a bagged mix that was originally intended to make biscuits, a staple where I come from, but with a little tweaking, this mix makes an excellent donut without a great deal of work.

You can make plain donuts with the blend straight out of the bag if you'd like, or you can add your favorite dried fruit, like cranberries or raisins. Chocolate chips for baking, whether dark or semisweet, also work well. My favorite lately is a combination of dried cranberries and dark chocolate chips.

It's amazing how well those flavors go together, so if you'd like a treat and don't have anything on hand, this is a great way to go!

Ingredients

1 packet (7 oz.) biscuit mix

2 1/2 tablespoons granulated sugar

1/2 cup whole milk

1/3 cup dried cranberries (raisins will work as well)

3 tablespoons semisweet chocolate chips

confectioners' sugar for dusting the tops of the donuts after they are fried

Directions

Heat enough canola oil in a pot to fry your donuts at 375 degrees F.

While you are waiting for the oil to come to temperature, take a medium-sized bowl and add the biscuit mix packet, sugar, and milk, mixing just long enough to combine the ingredients and get out most of the lumps.

Next, add the cranberries and chocolate chips, mixing in lightly until incorporated in the batter.

When your oil is at the correct temperature, drop small balls the size of your thumb into the hot oil, frying for approximately 3 to 5 minutes, turning halfway.

Remove from oil and let drain on paper towels, and then eat as is, or dust with confectioners' sugar if so desired.

Makes 10 to 11 small donuts

White Chicken Chili Soup

This has become a favorite in our household as of late. In fact, we've been known to have it three days in a row for lunch, adding any leftover shredded chicken and an extra can of Great Northern white beans to the mix whenever it needs to be stretched a bit. It's not just excellent on a cool autumn day; we like it when it's hot outside as well. The aromas coming from the stovetop when I'm making this dish are pure magic, and when it is coupled with some fresh homemade bread, it's enough to make my mouth water as I'm typing this!

Ingredients

1 medium white onion, diced

2 tablespoons olive oil (for sautéing the onions)

1 can chicken broth, organic (11 ounces)

2 cans Great Northern white beans, drained

1 chicken, hand pulled or shredded (I use a rotisserie chicken from the grocery store)

1 small can green chilis, chopped or diced

1 teaspoon salt

½ teaspoon oregano, dried

1/3 teaspoon cumin

a pinch to ¼ teaspoon cayenne (depending on how much heat you like)

½ cup sour cream

½ cup heavy whipping cream

Directions

Dice the onion and sauté it in the olive oil over medium heat. Once the onions are translucent, add the chicken stock, the beans, the pulled or shredded chicken, and the green chilis and stir.

Then add the salt, oregano, cumin, and cayenne and stir again. Bring the soup to a boil and simmer it over low heat for approximately 30 to 45 minutes.

Pull the pan from the heat and add the sour cream and whipping cream, stirring until it's mostly dissolved. Let this sit for 5 to 10 minutes and then serve.

TIP: You can heat up leftover soup in the microwave and it's just fine, but I like to do it on the stovetop, adding extra beans and chicken (if available) at that time.

Makes 6 adult-sized portions

Apple Cider Donuts

I'm not sure when you're reading this, but as I'm writing this recipe, autumn is definitely in the air. We've just returned from our annual trip to the orchard, where we pick up not only a great variety of apples, from Arkansas Black to Golden Blush to Granny Smith and more, while we're there, but we also grab fresh apple juice, apple cider, and of course, apple donuts! It's something the entire family looks forward to every year.

I always make sure to get enough cider to make these donuts, and heating the liquid gold on the stovetop not only adds a wonderful addition to the donuts themselves, but it makes the entire house smell like apples!

Ingredients

1 cup apple cider, fresh if you can get your hands on some

1/4 cup butter, room temperature

1 cup granulated sugar

2 eggs, beaten

1/2 cup buttermilk

4 cups all-purpose unbleached flour

2 teaspoons baking powder

1 teaspoon baking soda

1 teaspoon cinnamon

1 teaspoon nutmeg

1/2 teaspoon salt

For an optional glaze:

Confectioners' sugar

milk

Directions

Heat enough canola oil in a pot on your stovetop to 375 degrees. Make sure you have enough oil in the pot for the donuts to be submerged completely and rise to the top as they fry.

While you're waiting for the oil to heat, add the apple cider to a saucepan and heat it on the cooktop for about 10 minutes after it comes to a boil. To speed its cooling time, I like to put it in the refrigerator with a hotpad under the pan and cool it quickly, but if you want to let it cool naturally, don't start heating your oil until the cider is cooled.

In a large bowl, cream the butter and sugar together until smooth. Next, beat in the eggs, add the buttermilk and apple cider, and stir thoroughly.

In a medium-sized bowl, sift together the flour, baking powder, baking soda, cinnamon, nutmeg, and salt.

Slowly add the dry ingredients to the wet and mix until it forms a workable dough, adding more flour or buttermilk until you get the consistency desired. Roll out the dough to approximately ¼ inch thick, and then cut out into rounds, squares, or whatever shape suits your fancy!

Fry the donuts for approximately 3 to 5 minutes or until they are brown on each side, flipping them about halfway through the process.

Don't overcrowd the pot. It is better to do more smaller batches than large ones, but don't forget to let the oil come back up to heat between fryings.

Drain the donuts on paper towels and then dust them with powdered sugar, or make a simple glaze with confectioners' sugar and milk if so desired.

Makes 12 to 18 donuts, depending on the shapes and sizes you make.

If you enjoy Jessica Beck Mysteries and you would like to be notified when the next book is being released, please visit our website at jessicabeckmysteries.net for valuable information about Jessica's books, and sign up for her new-releases-only mail blast.

Your email address will not be shared, sold, bartered, traded, broadcast, or disclosed in any way. There will be no spam from us, just a friendly reminder when the latest book is being released, and of course, you can drop out at any time.

Other Books by Jessica Beck

The Donut Mysteries
Glazed Murder
Fatally Frosted
Sinister Sprinkles
Evil Éclairs
Tragic Toppings
Killer Crullers
Drop Dead Chocolate
Powdered Peril
Illegally Iced
Deadly Donuts
Assault and Batter
Sweet Suspects
Deep Fried Homicide
Custard Crime
Lemon Larceny
Bad Bites
Old Fashioned Crooks
Dangerous Dough
Troubled Treats
Sugar Coated Sins
Criminal Crumbs
Vanilla Vices
Raspberry Revenge
Fugitive Filling
Devil's Food Defense
Pumpkin Pleas
Floured Felonies
Mixed Malice

Tasty Trials
Baked Books
Cranberry Crimes
Boston Cream Bribes
Cherry Filled Charges
Scary Sweets
Cocoa Crush
Pastry Penalties
Apple Stuffed Alibies
Perjury Proof
Caramel Canvas
Dark Drizzles
Counterfeit Confections
Measured Mayhem
Blended Bribes
Sifted Sentences
The Classic Diner Mysteries
A Chili Death
A Deadly Beef
A Killer Cake
A Baked Ham
A Bad Egg
A Real Pickle
A Burned Biscuit
The Ghost Cat Cozy Mysteries
Ghost Cat: Midnight Paws
Ghost Cat 2: Bid for Midnight
The Cast Iron Cooking Mysteries
Cast Iron Will
Cast Iron Conviction
Cast Iron Alibi
Cast Iron Motive

Cast Iron Suspicion
Nonfiction
The Donut Mysteries Cookbook

Made in the USA
Middletown, DE
05 January 2020